From his position wa
stories of the aban

he had a really good view o
activity that was taking par
ban desert.

The view through the rifle's scope brought that activity into much clearer focus.

He was lying atop the padded shooting mat he had brought with him, along with the rifle and all its accessories.

The weapon was a 7.62mm ex-military M21 of the Vietnam War era. It was the US military's designated marksman, or sniper, rifle of the time, being little more than a slightly customised M14 battle rifle with a scope and bipod added.

After a long trudge through the upper levels many hours before, he had found a near-perfect hide for himself, a place where part of the low exterior wall had crumbled away to provide a small opening through which he could look and fire.

He aligned the scope onto one of the two vehicles parked out in the wilderness—a large, black SUV—and did some fine tuning until the image became crystal clear. He panned the scope away from the vehicle to his right eastwards toward the river until he came to the small scrap of orange tape fastened to one of the many rusted steel reinforcing bars that sprang up from the jumble of concrete slabs. Although it looked innocuous enough, the small piece of tape that fluttered in the steady breeze coming in off the river was not there by accident. He had risked trekking across the concrete wasteland at first light in order to tie it in place. It was his wind indicator.

Satisfied that the wind had hardly changed since his last check, he swung the rifle back toward the waiting vehicles to the battered old pickup this time, and to the large, imposing figure of the Indian who stood before it.

The scope he was using employed mil dot markings on the crosshair lines, and he began to put these to use now to accurately gauge the range. He put the horizontal cross hair directly in line with the top of the Indian's head, and counted down the mil dots to the bottom of his boots. It came out at 2.4.

Now he used the standard calculation of taking the size of the target in yards—he had seen the Indian fairly close up and put him to be six-four or thereabouts, which gave him 2.1 yards—and multiplying it by 1,000. This gave him 2,100. The final step in the formula was to divide this by the mil reading he had taken—2.4. This gave him a distance to the target of 875 yards. It was a long shot, and getting close to the rifle's maximum effective range, but he had every confidence in both the firearm and his own shooting ability.

Having established the range, he consulted the range card that he had painstakingly built up for the rifle and ammunition combination over the years. His ammunition was hand-loaded by himself to ensure maximum accuracy. He was using a Sierra .308 diameter Hollow Point Boat Tail, Match King bullet weighing 175 grains that, with the same carefully measured amount of propellant behind it, would consistently deliver a muzzle velocity of 2,600 feet per second.

The rifle was set to zero for 100 yards To compensate for bullet drop over longer distances, he would have to adjust the sight accordingly.

The card showed an elevation of 7.8 mil for 850 yards and 8.6 mil for 900. He split the difference and decided on a setting of 8.2, beginning to crank the elevation dial atop the scope counter-clockwise until he reached the desired setting.

He had already made adjustments to the scope's windage setting earlier based on what he calculated the wind strength and direction to be.

Now, he settled himself down into a comfortable shooting position and lowered his head to the stock again, finding the figure of the Indian in the scope once more, and centering the crosshairs into the middle of his upper chest. He began to regulate his breathing, taking up the first pressure on the trigger as he did so, and was only a second or two away from actually taking the shot when he heard the ominous double-click of a weapon being cocked immediately behind his left ear. The next instant, there was something cold and hard being pressed sharply into the back of his head.

The Movie Buff

Daniel Cassidy

Whimsical Publications, LLC

Florida

The Movie Buff is a work of fiction. Names, characters, and incidents are the products of the author's imagination and are either fictitious or are used fictitiously. Any resemblance to actual events or persons, living or dead, is entirely coincidental.

If you purchased this book without a cover, you should be aware that this book may have been stolen property and reported as "unsold and destroyed" to the publisher. In such case, neither the publisher nor the author has received payment for this "stripped book."

To purchase the authorized electronic edition of *The Movie Buff*, visit
www.whimsicalpublications.com

Cover art by Traci Markou
Editing by Brieanna Robertson

ISBN-13: 978-1-940707-20-4

Published by
Whimsical Publications, LLC
Florida

Acknowledgements

First and foremost, I would like to thank Janet Durbin—along with all the other good folk at Whimsical for giving me the chance to fulfil a lifelong ambition.

A special vote of thanks also to the book's editor—Brieanna Robertson—who taught me (among other things) the importance of maintaining POV. My thanks for the excellent editing job she did (and also for connecting some of the more obscure movie references).

I would also like to pass on my thanks to Paul Mcdonald of Mcdonald Armouries, Edinburgh, for his kind use of one of Mcdonald Armouries excellent F-S fighting knives as portrayed on the cover, and for providing me with much-needed information about the production and characteristics of the original knives. And also for saving me from making some embarrassing blunders—I now know the difference between 'etching' and 'engraving'. Many thanks Paul.

Finally, my greatest thanks (along with all my love) must go to my beautiful wife—Evelyn—for all the loving encouragement she—as always - provided, during the writing of the book. For not only listening to the daily 'updates' as it were, but for encouraging me (perhaps exhorting would be a better word) to increase both the quantity and the frequency of said excerpts.

Any writer struggling to meet a deadline should have an 'Evelyn' behind them.

This one is for the rocks upon which I have built my life—my darling wife Evelyn, our three loving sons—Steven, Sean and Nathan, and our wonderful grandsons—Liam and Daniel. God bless you all!

Chapter One

As places of residence go, the apartment block was a pretty shitty one, but seeing as it was located in a pretty shitty part of the city, that was really only to be expected.

As shitty as the building itself was, and as shitty as some of the other apartments within no doubt were, Connor's apartment was a good deal shittier than most. And he would probably be one of the first to admit that it was so.

He did not even pay lip service to the concept of clean and tidy.

One might have been forgiven for thinking that somebody had recently traipsed through the apartment, maliciously scattering the contents of several large garbage liners onto the floors and most of the surfaces of the tiny rooms.

The truth was, however, that the discarded food wrappers and empty beer and other cans that littered the floor and covered most of the furniture had never *seen* the inside of a garbage liner. Instead, they had been idly tossed away once their contents had been all—or partly—consumed.

Connor didn't give a shit. It soon would cease to be his problem. He wouldn't be in the place that much longer. He had just the one last brick to offload, just one final deal to conclude, and then he'd be free to leave, and leave he would—in a Goddamn New York minute.

He'd head south to warmer climates, maybe back to the heat of New Mexico, away from this crappy little apartment—an apartment that had become even more of a prison cell than the last fucking *real* cell he was in—and away from the whole friggin' city—a city full of nothing but cold and nut-jobs.

He took a final bite from the candy bar he was holding and tossed it away behind his back. There was still a decent chunk of chocolate left inside the wrapper and he heard the metallic *clunk* as it landed atop a beer or coke can.

He was sitting on just about the only piece of furniture that wasn't liberally coated with the detritus of his desperately unhealthy lifestyle—a large, threadbare but very comfortable easy chair that faced the one concession to luxury that the apartment contained—a 42-inch, flat-screen TV. It was the only Goddamn thing that was keeping him sane in his self-imposed confinement.

The movie he had been watching had just come to a close, and he was reaching for the remote to search for something else that was halfway decent, when the screen suddenly went blank.

Shit! Surely the damn thing couldn't be busted? I only bought the fucker a couple of weeks ago!

He reached across to the table lamp alongside him, having first to clear empty cans and candy wrappers out of the way to locate the switch on the cord. He flipped it on. Nothing.

A Goddamn power cut then. At least it isn't the TV.

With a sigh of weary resignation, he hauled himself from the chair and crossed to the room's only window, pulling the heavy drapes open just enough to verify that there were lights showing in the apartment block opposite. It wasn't full dark yet, but it was getting there.

It was just this building then. Little wonder. The place is so old and crummy that the wiring was probably done by fucking Edison.

Reluctantly, he drew the drapes wide, allowing the last of the fading daylight to illuminate what it could inside the darkened room.

He tried the phone, but, as expected, it too was dead.

The super will know anyway, surely? His own power will be out too. But what if it isn't? What if it is just this floor? Or even worse, just this apartment?

With a generous smattering of curses, he crunched his way back to the window, kicking aluminium cans and pizza boxes out of his way as he went. With a good deal of effort, he managed to raise the window, making the ancient wood whine and squeal in protest as he hauled the sash up high enough to create a gap that he could stick his head through.

He looked to the windows right and left and cursed at what he saw—there were lights shining behind most of them.

Fuck! It probably is *just my apartment then*. He would

have to go down and report it to the senile old prick.

He debated taking the Diamondback with him, and then decided against it. The damn thing was so friggin' big it would mean putting on a topcoat to conceal it.

Crossing to the door, he unlocked it, which was no simple task seeing as he had supplemented the original, flimsy Yale with a pair of much more substantial dead bolts, as well as a sturdy steel lockbar. When the door was finally open, he stepped outside into the dingy hallway, noting that the wall-mounted lights out there were still working.

He was halfway through locking the door behind him when he heard the approaching footsteps. He felt a blast of ice-cold dread shoot through his veins and was already berating himself for leaving the gun behind as he looked along the hallway to his right, where the footsteps were approaching from.

He let out a sigh of relief and cursed himself for being so jumpy. It was just some old fart of a maintenance guy wearing faded blue coveralls and carrying a battered steel toolbox.

"Don't tell me," the old guy said, holding his free hand up in front of him as if to ward off the expected words. "Yours is out too, right?"

Connor nodded in affirmation as he began to unlock the door again. "Yeah, what's the problem?" he asked.

"Well, we ain't completely sure yet, captain, but we think it's those blasted Diluthium crystals on the blink again." This was delivered in a terrible attempt at a Scottish accent.

Jesus, everybody in this whole fucking nut-job city is a wannabe comedian.

He threw the maintenance man a look of withering contempt that caused the old guy to give a fatalistic shrug and back off some with the humor.

"Guess we'll know better when you get me inside for a look at your fuse box," he said, reaching into his toolbox and pulling out a flashlight in readiness.

Connor opened up and they both went in.

"Jesus, did something die in here?" the old fuck asked, wrinkling his nose as he turned on the flash to sweep it around the room. The beam bounced erratically across the wasteland of discarded food wrappings and drink cans. "Dear lord, what a holy friggin' mess!"

"Yeah, well it's my cleaning lady's month off," Connor said. "Now, did you come to get the power back on or write an article for *The Happy Homes Review*?"

"Sonny, if this was my place, I'd just as soon keep it in the dark. You know all this crap is likely to encourage vermin, don't you?"

"Jeez, what are you, a fucking electrician or the Goddamn City Health Inspector? Just get the friggin' power back on why don't you?"

"I ain't an electrician. I'm just a handyman, and the power can wait another minute or two," the maintenance guy said. He placed his toolbox down atop the small mountain of debris that littered a nearby coffee table and reached inside it for something. He turned back then stepped in closer; suddenly, the intense whiteness of the flashlight's beam was hitting Connor full in the face, momentarily blinding him.

"Here, hold on to this for me," the old guy said, and then punched him hard in the midriff.

Connor let out a whoosh of pained surprise as he felt the air being driven from his body. The maintenance guy was right on top of him now, pushing him backwards across the carpet of garbage that littered the room.

Connor tried to resist, but for an old feller, the maintenance guy was surprisingly strong, and he felt himself propelled backwards until the back of his legs came up against the seat of the easy chair, causing his knees to fold and buckle. He sank back and down into the familiar softness of the old cushions, letting out another grunt of pain as he did so.

His stomach was still on fire from where the old bastard had punched him, and he put his hands to his middle in an attempt to ease the hurt.

He felt it first, letting out a little terrified yelp of alarm as he did so. Then the flashlight's beam played across his midriff, and the yelp turned into a sobbing whimper as he beheld the handle of the knife that was protruding from his stomach. His shaking fingers curled around the slim, knurled metal handle.

"I'd leave it right where it is, if it was me," the old guy said.

His wise-ass city accent had suddenly vanished, and Connor now knew that he definitely wasn't a native of the place. In fact, he suddenly had serious doubts that the guy was even

American.

"Right now it's acting just like a plug," the man continued in a faintly disinterested tone, as though he were discussing the local weather. "You yank on that plug and you'll likely empty out within a minute or two, just like a bathtub. A thing like that needs to be removed at a hospital."

The word "hospital" rang out in Connor's confused mind.

Hospital? The old fuck was talking about hospitals. That was good, wasn't it? Maybe he hadn't been sent to take him out?

And then his eyes were drawn back to that slim, elegantly-shaped knife hilt that was sticking straight out of his middle, and the anger came bubbling to the surface.

"You stabbed me, you crazy old fucker!" Connor exclaimed, his hands now clasped to his belly but careful to leave the knife in place. "Why the fuck did you stab me?"

"Because I didn't want to make too much noise shooting you, but I will if I have to."

The flashlight had by this time been placed alongside the toolbox on the coffee table, and by the light it threw off, Connor could see that there was now a small, nickel-plated semi-automatic pistol in the man's right hand.

"Don't let the size fool you," the maintenance guy said, except by now Connor very much doubted that was what the old coot actually was.

"It's only a little .22, I know, but if I put one in your eye—and from this distance, that won't be a problem, believe me—it'll do just as good as a .44 magnum."

"Why'd you fucking stab me?" Connor repeated.

"I already answered that. If you mean, why did I 'attack' you, it's because you really shouldn't have done what you did."

"Who sent you? Was it the Cooper boys?"

The old guy didn't answer, just began reaching into his toolbox to withdraw a large roll of duct tape. Connor could see where that was going. He took in a great breath ready to yell for help before it did.

"Don't!" the man advised, moving unbelievably quickly to place the barrel of the tiny pistol to Connor's lips. "If you open your mouth again before I'm ready for you to, I'll put a bullet through it. Besides, in this shithole, who's gonna take notice of a few yells?"

Connor let the breath come back out through his nostrils in a soft exhalation of defeat.

Five minutes later, breathing through his nostrils was the only option open to him. The duct tape had been used to great effect to not only gag him, but also to bind him securely to the easy chair. The old guy had not stinted on its use, and the empty cardboard cylinder now lay atop the other accumulated rubbish at Connor's feet. As a consequence, Connor was now as tightly wrapped as an Egyptian mummy.

"There, that should hold you for a spell, I guess," the old guy said as he walked around the chair to inspect his handiwork.

Satisfied, he began to make his way to the door.

Connor began to panic.

Oh Jesus, is the crazy old fucker just gonna leave me here? The rent was all paid up for three months in advance. Sweet Jesus, it could be another ten fucking weeks before anyone found him!

As if sensing his thoughts, the old guy turned back to face him.

"Don't worry, I won't be long. Just need to re-set that trip switch and get some power back on in here." With that, he was out the door, locking it behind him as he left.

Connor's mind was in turmoil. Who the fuck was the bastard? More importantly, who had sent him? Somebody had fingered him and set him up, of that he was certain. Was it the Coopers? Were they simply trying to make the deal without losing any more outlay? Is that why they had kept him waiting so long? Or had the crazy little Irish prick or maybe even the Indian set him up? Surely, the Cubans hadn't been able to track him down?

These questions, along with a myriad of others, were still bouncing around his skull when the flat screen burst back into life and the table lamp lit up.

Minutes later, the old guy was back in the room and kneeling beside him. None too gently, the duct tape around his mouth was removed.

"Who the fuck *are* you?" Connor asked as soon as he was able.

"I told you, I'm just a handyman. I fix things. I'm fixing things right now for an old friend."

"There's money," Connor blurted. "As well as the powder.

You can have it all."

"I'm not interested in your money. I know how you most likely earned it. I will take the powder, though. Where is it?"

Connor told him. He left the room and went into the apartment's tiny kitchen to retrieve it. There was a full brick of it wrapped tightly in brown wax paper.

The man removed a folding knife from his pocket and flipped the blade open with his thumb. Watching him, Connor noted for the first time that he was wearing thin latex gloves.

He used a foot to clear the rubbish away from a patch of stained, threadbare carpet, and laid the brick in the middle of the space he had created. He bent and used the knife to slit open the package. The blade, though small, was very sharp, and the heavy brown paper parted easily.

The old guy stood back up, unzipped his fly, took out his penis, and proceeded to urinate on the small brick of white powder at his feet.

"You're fuckin' *crazy*!" Connor whispered in awe as he watched the fucker literally piss away thousands of dollars worth of high-quality product.

With the powder on the carpet reduced to a steaming puddle of yellow gunk, the old guy gave his penis a few last shakes before putting it back in his pants. "Sorry about the mess," he said with a slight smile.

"Oh Jesus, stop it please," Connor said, unable to control his anger at the waste. "You're fuckin' crackin' me up, man, and it really hurts when I laugh!"

"You're right," the old guy said. "This is no time for levity. I guess now that the power is back on, we can get started." He crossed to the toolbox and produced another—this time smaller—roll of duct tape.

Connor guessed—correctly—what was coming, and a minute or two later was sitting there efficiently gagged again.

He watched the man replace the unused tape back in the box and then cross to the wall where the table lamp was plugged in. He removed the plug from the socket. The little sharp folding knife came into play again, and he used the blade to cut the wire away from the base of the lamp. Then, with quick, deft motions, he used the knife to trim away the insulation from the ends of the two wires.

There was another dip into the toolbox and the man's hand came out brandishing a pair of large scissors.

Connor watched in terrified fascination as the old bastard came closer and began to cut away first his trousers and then his underpants.

Oh Jesus-fuck no! The crazy old fucker is going to snip my dick off!

He mumbled and moaned into the gag, desperately shaking his head in denial.

He almost fainted with relief when he saw the man place those wicked-looking shears back into the toolbox, then produce in their place a pair of crocodile clips.

He brought over the cable that he had cut away from the lamp, and braided one of the bared wires on to each clip. Then he opened up the jaws of one clip and reached forward to attach it to the metal handle of the knife that was firmly embedded in Connor's stomach.

Connor's heart began to triphammer in alarm, and the next instant, his worse fears were confirmed as the second clip was quickly applied to his shrunken scrotum. He hissed in pain and alarm as the wicked, serrated edges bit into the folds of wrinkled skin.

"Why? Why are you fucking doing this?" Connor screamed into the confines of the tape that covered his mouth, and although the words were more or less unintelligible, the old man picked up on their meaning.

"I came down here from Philly," he told Connor. "Right after visiting with your nasty friend Farrell."

Farrell! He had been right then. That evil little Irish prick had fingered him to this fucking old nut-job. But if that were so, why hadn't he taken the powder to deliver to him?

"You're wanting to know why, I can see that," the man continued in that same reasoned, friendly tone. "I already told you. You shouldn't have done what you did, not to a helpless little girl."

Oh sweet Jesus, was that what this was all about? Not the money, the powder, the Cubans, or the fucking Coopers?

"She knew Farrell. Did he tell you that? He used to come into her father's store."

Oh motherfucker! That dumb Irish bastard!

"The little girl gave me Farrell, and—after a bit of persuasion—he gave me you."

That caused Connor to wonder just what that "persuasion" had involved. The little Irish fucker was as crazy as a bedbug—he had proven that beyond all doubt down in Florida and again back in Philly—and did not scare or rattle easily.

Connor mumbled and muttered into the gag, wanting desperately to tell the man that it hadn't been him. It was Farrell. Farrell had picked the girl up, snatched her right off the street, and had brought her back to them. Well, okay, he and the Indian had both taken their turns, it was true. Jesus, he could hardly fucking remember it—they had all been as high as friggin' kites—but it had been Farrell who had beaten her senseless and done the worst things to her. Christ, none of it would have happened if not for Farrell.

The old guy just ignored Connor's frantic mumblings and picked up the TV remote from the armrest of the chair. He flipped through the channels until he found an old Western movie, then adjusted the volume until the noise of gunfire and yelling Apaches filled the room.

"I said I wasn't an electrician, and I'm not, but I'm going to have a go at playing one for a couple of minutes or so." As he was speaking, he moved across the room until he was adjacent to the wall socket where the lamp cable had been plugged in. "After that, we can take your gag back off, and you'll give me the third bastard—the Indian. The one that Farrell couldn't tell me too much about."

He reached down to the plug.

Connor was already screaming, or trying to, before he even got it into the socket.

Chapter Two

It had been a stroke of pure luck that SAC Jim Clarkson was in the city at the time. Though later, when it was all over, he would come to question whether it had been a question of good luck or bad.

Both he and his new assistant—Special Agent Joseph Martin, who had transferred to the unit from the DEA—were attending a week-long anti-drug seminar laid on by one of the state's leading universities, and attended by law enforcement personnel from all over the globe.

In Clarkson and Martin's case, attendance had not been up for discussion. They had been instructed to attend, along with a great many other agents and officers from the new unit.

The unit CADI—the Combined Anti-Drug Initiative—was still in its infancy. It had been formed from component parts of the three main Federal agencies tasked with the reduction of drug trafficking and drug-related crime—the FBI, the DEA, and ICE.

The formation had been largely due to political pressure and posturing—all three agencies had come in for a great amount of criticism in the past for their high-handed, elitist behavior, along with their reluctance to share information with each other.

It was felt by some high-rankers in the current administration that the pooling together of personnel and resources from all three agencies to act as a central conduit for the passing and sharing of information would go a long way to remedying the situation and making the war on drugs that much more effective.

It was felt by nearly everyone else, including most of the nation's media, along with a fair percentage of the people drafted into the new agency, that it would prove to be just another huge money-leech on the country's dwindling financial resources and would provide the possibility for yet another FSCF—Federal-Sized Cluster-Fuck.

Nevertheless, for the time being, the CADI was beginning to swing into full nation-wide operation, taking Clarkson and his small team of operatives along with it.

Truth be told, when the call came from the newly set up regional office via the local PD, both Clarkson and Martin had been glad to be called away from the seminar. It had proven to be intensely boring with very little new ground or procedures being covered. Most of the stuff being discussed had been picked up by Clarkson during his first few months with the FBI, and that had been a coon's age ago and then some. Even some of the new "revelations," such as the employment of fake TV unit vans, Fed-Ex, and even Border Patrol trucks to transport narcotics in were pretty old hat.

The call that had pulled them out of the seminar—for now at least—had come as part of the new, nation-wide directive to automatically alert the CADI to any new criminal cases that involved the discovery of large quantities of narcotics.

Now, as he stepped through the doorway into the apartment, Clarkson wasn't so sure that he wouldn't prefer being bored shitless back at the seminar.

The stench inside the place was definitely something to write home about.

He reached inside his topcoat to retrieve his handkerchief and held it to his lower face. A glance to his rear showed him that Martin was doing the same.

The apartment's main room was somewhat crowded to say the least, mostly by numerous tech guys in white coveralls and face masks. Clarkson couldn't help but envy them their masks.

He approached the small knot of people clustered around the body in the easy chair, managing to get a quick glimpse before one of the technicians wheeled around and held up a gloved hand to stop him. The guy mumbled something unintelligible into his mask, and though he couldn't make out the words, the tone in which they were spoken, along with the angry flash in the speaker's eyes, told Clarkson he was not being welcomed to the party.

He held up his hands in apology and stepped back a pace or two, his shoes crunching through the litter underfoot. He felt his right sole squelch into a patch of stickiness, and then felt the adhesive resistance as he tried to raise his foot again. He looked down in disgust at the strands of gunk that were now strung out between his shoe and the floor, and muttered a hard curse into his handkerchief.

His angry muttering caught the attention of the one person in the room not wearing a white forensic outfit—a tall, lean-framed black man wearing a fashionable, if slightly rumpled, navy blue suit. The man held one of the crime scene guys' disposable masks to his face. He looked at Clarkson and pointed back toward the apartment's doorway, then followed the two agents as they made their way back out.

Outside in the relative freshness of the hallway, Clarkson pocketed his handkerchief and introduced himself and Martin.

"Kinda figured that's who you were," the man said, bringing the mask from his face and wrapping its elastic band around his wrist a couple of times. He offered his hand to each agent in turn and gave them a brief but firm handshake.

"Tom Laurence—lieutenant, local homicide. The CSA boys are going to be a while, probably best not to disturb them too much at this point. I can bring you up on the major details while we wait."

Clarkson nodded in agreement.

"Victim was the apartment's registered resident. Moved in about three weeks ago. Registered in the name of Donald Fisher, though that's probably not his real name. We found three other sets of different ID in his belongings. Given what else we found in there and the fact that he has a fair number of 'jailhouse' tattoos showing on what we can currently see of his body, I'm betting he's got himself a record somewhere. Fingerprints will tell us soon enough."

"What else did you find?" Clarkson asked.

"Well, there's the dope obviously, otherwise you boys wouldn't be here," Laurence said.

Clarkson nodded and asked, "How much?"

"Well, it's kinda hard to tell, given its present state, but the lab boys reckon at least a kilo."

"Its present state?" Clarkson repeated.

"Yeah, it ain't much more than a lumpy yellow stain on the carpet now, on account of somebody taking a leak all over it."

"You're shitting me," Clarkson said, but Laurence shook

his head to show that he wasn't.

"You mean to tell me that somebody took a piss all over twenty K's worth of product?"

"That's what the lab guys are saying, yes," Laurence confirmed.

"What else was in there?"

"Well, nothing that would point to Mr. Fisher—if that *is* his real name—being up for any local good citizenship awards. There was upwards of fifty grand in cash stashed in the freezer, and a Diamondback DB15 pistol, along with a couple of fully-loaded clips, in one of the dresser drawers."

Clarkson was not familiar with the model and raised his eyebrows in question.

"It's basically a chopped down AR-15," Laurence stated, pulling out his phone and finger-swiping the screen until he found what he was looking for. He turned the phone around to show Clarkson the image.

"You're shitting me," Clarkson said again. "That thing qualifies as a fucking pistol? It's a Goddamn assault rifle."

"Won't get an argument from me," Laurence countered. "Guess it's the seven-and-a-half inch barrel that swings it. Fucker fires a full .223 rifle round, though, and can take a twenty or even thirty-round magazine."

"Jesus, these fuckers are better friggin' armed than we are."

"Again, no argument here."

"What about cause of death?" Clarkson asked. He was gratified to notice that off to the side Martin was busy taking notes. They had not known each other that long, having more or less been thrown together only a week or so before, but the kid did seem to show promise. "Was it the stab wound?"

"You saw that, huh?" Laurence said. "The medical officer thinks not, but won't commit himself just yet. The thinking is that that was done as either punishment or to retrieve information. I'm guessing you saw the wires?"

Clarkson nodded.

"We got close-proximity powder burn marks on the victim's right ear and a fair-sized exit wound on the other side of the guy's head. That, coupled with a decent amount of blood and brain tissue on the adjacent wall, leaves us with an obvious gunshot wound to the head, probably with a small caliber pistol—possibly a .22. We'll know for sure when the lab guys dig the slug out of the wall. The gunshot could have been post-mortem, of course, but then why would somebody put a bullet through the brain of a guy that's already dead?"

"Maybe for the same reason that somebody would piss over a block of coke worth twenty grand," Clarkson answered. "Namely because the guy is probably an out-and-out whacko. At this stage, I'm not prepared to rule anything out on this one."

Laurence gave Clarkson a long, hard look before saying, "Agent, we need to get one thing absolutely clear from the get-go here. This homicide is *mine*—mine and the city's. The drugs and anything related to their import and distribution is yours. Do we understand that?"

Clarkson was equally frank with his look back at the lieutenant before answering. "First off, lieutenant, I am *not* an agent. I'm a Special Agent in Charge—there is a *world* of fucking difference. Second, anything related to a kilo block of cocaine, even one that's been pissed on, is mine. And I am going to take that to include any dead bodies that are found in the immediate vicinity of said cocaine. The homicide inside that apartment is going to be a prime feature of our investigations into this matter. Needless to say, any information that we uncover along the way that relates to criminal activities within the confines of your own fair city will be passed along to you. I think our first priority here should be to apprehend this nut-job before he can wire anybody else up to the friggin' mains and then apply a firearms-induced lobotomy. After that, we can argue about who should deal with him and how. Don't you agree?"

Laurence gave a curt, and obviously reluctant, nod.

"I'm guessing nobody heard the shot?" Clarkson continued.

"Nobody who wants to admit to it," the lieutenant said. "To be fair, the TV *was* playing kinda loud. One of the reasons the body was actually discovered. Somebody complained to the super that the damn thing was blaring away twenty-four hours through. He came up to investigate, couldn't get an answer and opened up the mail slot to try and take a look-see. When he got a whiff of what we've just been inhaling, he called it in."

"Do we have a time frame?"

"The medical officer is putting it at three, maybe four

days ago."

"What about all the crud in there?" Clarkson asked. "Why would someone empty out all that garbage like that? Think they were expecting to find something hidden in the trash bags?"

"It's not like that," Laurence explained. "The analysts say the garbage is layered. The stuff underneath has been there longer than the crap on top. They think the dead guy was just a 24-carat slob, is all. Eating and drinking stuff and just tossing away the wrappers and cans. There ain't a garbage sack in the place, not a used one anyways. Hell, the kitchen is probably the cleanest room in the whole friggin' apartment."

Clarkson looked incredulous. "Jesus, can people actually live like that?"

"I guess you ain't done too much of your police work in big cities, huh?" Laurence replied.

Clarkson let it go. "Once your CSI boys are done, we're going to need to get back in there before they remove the body," he said, noting the low moan from Martin behind him in reaction to his words.

"We don't have CSI boys—that's a TV show," the lieutenant said. "And I don't know why you'd want to go back in. You'll have full access to all the photos and other reports."

"I don't want access to *photographs*. I want access to a crime scene where a whole friggin' kilo of cocaine was discovered. Just let me know when we can get back in."

Laurence raised his hands in defeat. "Not a problem," he said. "It's your evening meal being ruined, I guess." He turned to re-enter the apartment.

"Oh, and lieutenant." Clarkson stopped him in his tracks, and the detective turned around with a look of weary resignation on his face.

"Yes?"

"See if you can organize a loan of a couple of those friggin' masks, will you?"

For the first time since they had shaken hands, the homicide detective smiled at him.

Chapter Three

To be honest, the masks didn't help that much, even with a liberal dosing of the cheap aftershave that Martin had discovered in the bathroom cabinet.

The spectacle of the body in the chair, especially when coupled with the all-pervading stench, was not particularly pleasing either, and Martin knew that the lieutenant would prove to be right. His evening meal that night was not something he would be looking forward to. After his first initial close-up inspection at SAC Clarkson's insistence, he had retreated as far back as was prudent without giving the impression of his being overly squeamish.

In contrast, Clarkson had now moved in as close to the body as was possible, and was now actually squatting down in front of it, tapping the side of his head with a small, gold-plated ballpoint as he studied the purplish, bloated remains of what had once been a man.

Clarkson lifted his mask slightly away from his face in order to speak.

"You know, when I first came in earlier, I was thinking *Seven*, or maybe even *Saw*. But now I ain't so sure. I think I have seen this one, though" he said, reaching out to use the end of the pen to lift away the wire that was still attached to what remained of the corpse's genitals.

"Sir?" was all that Martin could answer.

"You like the movies, son?" Clarkson asked, throwing Martin completely off guard.

"Movies, sir?"

"Sure, you know, movies—Hollywood. Big screen entertainment."

"Well, sure, I guess. Whenever there's anything decent playing." Martin did not have a clue where this was going, and furthermore, he felt like an idiot having to constantly lift the mask from his face in order to speak like a jazz trumpeter using a mute.

"What was this one called?" his supervisor asked, still dangling the wire in the air away from the strapped-down body.

Jesus! How could he stand to be so fucking close to that thing?

"I'm sorry sir, I'm afraid you've lost me."

"C'mon, you must have seen it. The big Irish guy—what the fuck's his name? Played Rob Roy a while back. Now that was a fine movie, though I did think the skinny little English prick totally stole the show."

"Er, sir, I think Rob Roy was Scottish," Martin ventured.

"Of course he was. Did I say he wasn't?"

"But you said *Irish*. Big *Irish* guy is what you said."

"Jeez, I'm talking about the *actor,* not Rob-fucking-Roy! You *must* have seen it, what the fuck was it called? Kidnapped, something like that. The big guy's daughter is on a visit to Europe, and gets kidnapped by some low-life bunch of eastern European slave traders. But they bit off more than they could chew, see, because the big guy—Jesus, what the *fuck* is his name? Well, anyway, he turns out to be ex-CIA, a real badass, you know? He tracks down one of these fuckers and nails him to a chair, then shoots electricity through the nails to get him to talk. Christ, Martin, you must have seen it."

Martin could only shake his head, now completely baffled as to where this was going. "Sir, you think the CIA is involved in this?" he asked, somewhat lamely.

Clarkson turned to look at him—a long, steady look that made Martin wish he had said nothing.

"Son, let's not get going on movies with plots about CIA involvement in criminal activities and murder conspiracies, otherwise we'll be here all friggin' night." He rose from his squat and came back across the room to stand beside Martin.

Martin was hoping that they would leave the apartment, but instead, Clarkson just stood there, looking all around him and bringing the little gold pen up to his temple again.

"Why?" He flung the question out into the putrefied atmosphere. "We got the how; we need to know *why*. Why would anyone do such a thing? Why would *you* do such a thing, Joseph?"

Martin was taken aback by the question. "Sir, I wouldn't,"

was all that he could manage in response.

"No?" Clarkson asked. "Not even if the bastard had just kidnapped your daughter?"

"Sir, I don't have a daughter."

Clarkson ignored him. "I think the lieutenant was right. When it comes down to it, there can only be two reasons—punishment or information. Revenge or knowledge. Or maybe it was both. Information about what, though? Certainly not anything related to financial gain. Who would torture a man to find out where the buried treasure lay only to walk away and leave nearly a hundred grand in cash and coke behind? Jesus, I wish I could remember that Irish guy's name."

He turned toward the doorway, and Martin heaved a sigh of relief into his mask as he made ready to follow. Instead of going through it, though, Clarkson stopped when he reached the door and toed it shut, cutting off what little flow of untainted air was coming into the place.

"Just take a look at that, will you?" Clarkson said, indicating the back of the door and its frame. "Guy's got the place locked up tighter than a snare drum, and he's sitting here armed with a mini-fucking-machine gun..."

"Sir, it's actually classified as a pistol," Martin dared to interrupt.

Clarkson gave him a look before sweeping his coat aside to reveal his belt-worn sidearm.

"Son, *this* is a pistol. It's a Glock 21 chambered for .45 ACP, which is a *pistol* round. What are you carrying?" he asked, sweeping the right of Martin's coat aside as he did so. There was nothing there, and he flipped his hand across to throw the left of Martin's coat to the side. Again, nothing. "Where's your friggin' piece at?"

"Sir, small of the back," Martin answered.

"Small of the friggin' back? What the hell for?"

"Well, I find it's less conspicuous there."

"Less conspicuous? What the fuck you need to be inconspicuous for? You're a Federal fucking agent, Goddammit. You can walk around with it strapped to the side of your fucking head if you want to! Get that changed, son, and pronto. We get into a fix of any kind, I don't want you dancing around with your hand up your butt trying to locate your friggin' gun while I'm waiting on some backup. What you carrying anyway, a nine?"

"No, sir, it's a Sig Pro in .40 S&W."

"Why, hell, that's a damn good choice, Joseph. Never had much use for a nine myself—friggin' worst move the military ever made ditching the old .45. Just get her hitched round to the front some, where it belongs. Anyway, back to what I was saying, 9mm, 10mm, .40 S&W, .45 Colt Auto, .357 and .44 mag—they're *all* pistol rounds designed to be fired from a friggin' pistol, right?"

Martin nodded his head, wondering if he could claim a new holster on expenses. His old one was designed exclusively for small-of-the-back carry.

"Now, the weapon that the nice policeman was kind enough to show us pictures of," Clarkson continued, "was chambered for the .223, which, if you recall, is a cartridge designed to be loaded into and fired from a fucking *rifle*. So getting back to what I was about to say before your interruption, here's our boy sitting real pretty behind a well-locked security door, got himself a mini-fucking-assault-rifle in his lap." He paused to see if Martin would give him any more argument. Martin wisely chose not to, and Clarkson continued. "And yet, whoever gets in here to do the terrible deed does so without busting the locks and without a damn shot from that friggin' wannabe pistola being fired." He paused to let Martin think about it for a second or two. "So, how do we explain that, Joseph?"

It was not that hard to work out. "The victim let him in, sir?"

"The victim let him in! Exactly, son. Now why the fuck would he do that, hmm?"

"Because he knew him, sir."

"Because he knew him." Clarkson nodded his head in agreement.

"Or..." Martin began.

"Yes?"

"Because he didn't feel threatened?"

Clarkson took the mask completely away from his face and beamed at Martin before reaching across to open the door.

Chapter Four

The precinct house office that had been allocated to them was not really that much of an office. It bore more resemblance to a broom-cupboard that had had a desk, telephone, and computer installed. It was a cheerless, windowless little space, small and confined to begin with, and now, with all the duplicate reports and copies of the crime scene photographs stacked up wherever there was space, it appeared to be even smaller.

Martin was sitting behind the room's only desk, working his way through one of the reports, when Clarkson came in carrying two Styrofoam coffee containers. Not surprisingly, given the room's lack of decent ventilation, his assistant had taken off his jacket and was working in shirtsleeve order. Clarkson was pleased to note the new, shiny black leather holster that now resided in a cross-draw position, only inches away from the belt buckle on the young agent's left side.

He pushed one of the coffees across to Martin, who grunted in thanks, and then picked up a pile of manila folders from the seat of the room's only other chair and repositioned them on the floor before sitting himself down.

"Anything new?" he asked.

"Couple of things," Martin said, popping the lid off his coffee cup. He took a sip and smiled in appreciation. "I'm guessing this ain't station house?"

"You kidding?" Clarkson countered. "You could stand a friggin' crowbar up in that stuff, never mind a spoon. I'm betting it's got a birthday coming up real soon. Had to walk almost a block for these. So, what we got?"

"Well, we got an ID on the body for one. Guy's name was Connor, David Connor. Laurence was right, he does have a sheet, and has seen the inside of more than one correctional facility, his latest being for minor drug offenses out in New Mexico. Got out just over a year ago. Since then, nothing." He took another sip of coffee and then reached across the cluttered desk for another folder. "The knife is interesting. We might well get somewhere with it. It's a Fairbairn-Sykes fighting knife. Unusual in that it has no other really practical application other than killing people. It was designed and developed out in China before WWII by a couple of guys who used to work for the Shanghai Municipal Police force. Guess things must have been a little rough back then in old Shanghai.

"The knife became famous during WWII when it was issued to the British Commando units, the SAS, and other Special Forces, including our own OSS. It's been copied fairly extensively, and several versions of it are still in production, so there are literally millions of them out there. But what makes ours so interesting is that it's one of the very early pattern ones, maybe even from the original batch made by Wilkinson Sword back in 1941."

"Which means?" Clarkson asked.

"Well, it isn't unique, but it's still a valuable and highly collectable item, not the kind of thing you'd be apt to come across on a regular basis out on the street."

"Which begs the question," Clarkson said, "if the damn thing is gonna prove to be so traceable, then why the hell was it left behind?"

"You think it's a deliberate red herring?" Martin asked.

"I don't know yet. What else we got?"

"Well, the medical officer's initial assessment proved to be true—cause of death, a gunshot wound to the head. Laurence was right about the caliber. The slug they recovered was a .22, no match on the ballistics database to any other crimes. The other gun, though, does have some history. The Diamondack DB15? We got database positives on that. Seems it was used in some kind of gangland shootout deemed to be drug related just over a month ago down in Florida. Four local guys, well known to the Florida police, found shot and dumped in the underbrush not far from a fairly secluded little cove. The beach would have made for an ideal drop point for a drug shipment. All of the victims suffered multiple gunshot wounds, all with high-velocity rounds that were mostly pass-throughs. Only two bullet heads were recovered, one from one of the bodies and one from the trunk of a nearby tree—both .223 and both fired from our boy's Diamondback."

"A drug hijacking, you think?" Clarkson asked.

"It's looking likely," Martin said. "It would certainly explain where the block of coke came from, along with the money that was found. It would also give us a motive—whoever was meant to receive that shipment is apt to be more than a little pissed about it."

"Yeah," Clarkson mused. "But what it wouldn't give us is a reason why whoever was sent to collect the payback was satisfied to just take payment out of Connor's hide, and leave the money behind after using twenty K's worth of coke as a friggin' toilet."

All that Martin could offer up to that was a resigned shrug.

"So, what else?" Clarkson asked.

"Well, the money recovered tots up to just over fifty-two grand," Martin answered. "Which would seem to indicate that if it was from drug sales, our Mr. Connor may have already passed on another three kilos or so." He picked up another slim folder and flipped through it until he found what he was looking for.

"Here's something curious. When the science guys had more or less nailed down the time of death, the beat guys went back in and re-questioned everyone in the apartments about the day and time in question. Mostly, they drew a blank, but there was one lady, a nurse at the local hospital who lives on the floor above, who remembers seeing, and almost colliding with, an old maintenance guy coming up the stairs as she was going down. She remembers it because she was on her way out to work and it was the day her shifts changed. When Laurence gets the report, he sends one of his boys back out there to question the maintenance guy, and—here's the funny thing..."

"There isn't a maintenance guy employed there," Clarkson finished for him.

"Laurence already told you about it, huh?" Martin said.

"Nope. Laurence didn't have to. Jeez, Joseph, you saw that place. You honestly think whoever owns it is gonna be paying out a steady wage to a maintenance guy? Fuck me, it's just as likely that they'd hire a friggin' doorman. Places like that the poor old super gets hit with all the shitty fix-it jobs that come along. Anything he can't handle either doesn't get fixed or he contracts out to a local handyman." He paused to lake a long swig of his coffee. "An old maintenance guy, huh?" he said, and then added, "Someone you wouldn't feel threatened by."

Martin had his own coffee cup halfway to his lips and put it back onto the desk without drinking. "Goddamn!" he whispered.

"So, you're sitting in a shithole of an apartment with an incriminating kilo block in your possession. Why would you open up, even for an innocuous-looking old maintenance guy?" Clarkson said.

Martin didn't have to think long. "Because something in the apartment needed fixing."

"And what in the apartment might an outside party be able to influence to go wrong?"

"The electrics!" Both men said in unison.

A half-hour later, they were back at the apartment building.

The super lead them down into the basement to the small utility cupboard that contained the building's main fuse boxes. The door was secured with a sturdy-looking steel hasp and small brass padlock, neither of which looked to have been tampered with.

"Is it always kept locked?" Clarkson asked.

"Damn right," the super said. "Think I want any of these clowns coming down here trying to rig up free juice for their pads?"

"Open her up," Clarkson said.

The super drew out his key ring and flipped through the numerous keys until he was satisfied he had the right one, then bent to unlock the padlock. There was a bit of fumbling and the jingle of the key ring again until finally, he rose back up, scratching at and shaking his head.

"Damn!" he said.

Clarkson smiled. "Don't tell me," he said. "Key don't fit no more."

Chapter Five

"So you think he wore a disguise then—make himself look old?" Laurence asked.

They were back in the crummy little closet of an office, which with the addition of the lieutenant's impressive frame, now seemed even smaller.

"What, you think only young guys can commit homicide?" Clarkson asked, and then before Laurence could answer, he went on. "Have you any idea how hard it would be for the average person to make himself up to look older? Convincingly, I mean? It isn't just a matter of slapping on a grey wig and walking with a stoop, you know. You got to stop watching those *Mission Impossible* movies, Tom. Those masks aren't real, you know. Truth is, it just isn't in most people's capability to change their appearance by throwing on a bit of makeup and a few bits and pieces of latex. That's a real professional's job. And when somebody untrained does try, the effects are usually downright obvious, and usually have the unwanted effect of drawing attention to the person in question. No, I think our guy is pretty near as old as he was making out to be. The nurse puts it at mid-sixties. At least now we have a slightly better idea of *who* we're looking for. The *why* is still a pretty long ways off, though."

"You did good work," Laurence acknowledged. "It might have been weeks before the super noticed the switch with those padlocks, and even then he might not have made the connection. The original padlock was sawn through—our tech guys found traces of the steel filings on the floor—and replaced with a near-identical one. Guy must have done reconnaissance beforehand to find out what kind of lock it was. This was a planned operation, almost military in the way it was carried out. We got our people looking at the replacement lock. No luck on prints, and it's a popular brand that you can pick up almost anywhere. No luck with prints on any of the fuse boxes and trip switches either."

"I kinda thought that might be the case," Clarkson said. "Joseph here is looking to access any similar torture-killings via the FBI's NCIC database. That could produce a lot of hits, though, and it follows the assumption that this guy has worked before using a similar M.O., which we don't know is actually true or not. We're also putting an official FBI query out to any Militaria and Edged Weapons dealers who might have sold an early Fairbairn-Sykes recently. Joseph was right, the knife is fairly distinctive, and early models don't come that cheap." As he was speaking, he had picked up a photograph of the knife in question. "That is one mean-looking piece of steel," he admitted. "I don't think I'd have called it a fighting knife, though."

"No, what would you call it?" Laurence asked.

"A Goddamn killing tool," Clarkson stated, and then carried on. "So, what we got here then, Tom, is a combat knife that was almost exclusively issued to Special Forces, an elderly guy who could well have put in some service in said forces, and a meticulously planned, near-military operation. You thinking what I'm thinking, Tom?"

"I guess you're thinking ex-military," Laurence said.

"No, Tom, what I'm thinking is First-fucking-Blood," Clarkson said. He swung an arm around to point at Martin behind his back. "And don't you go rolling your fucking eyes at me, Joseph!" he ordered, causing Martin—who had been doing exactly that—to almost spill the coffee that he was holding.

"Say what?" Laurence said.

"You know, *First Blood*? The Rambo film," Clarkson said.

"Which one?" Laurence countered. "There's a dozen of the fuckers."

"The *only* fucking one, as far as I'm concerned," Clarkson said. "The first one—the one that followed Morrell's book, or near as, damn it. Now that was a damn fine book. Turned into a damn fine move too, despite having fucking Rocky in the title role. Brian Dennehy acted his socks off, though, as usual. Now *there's* a guy who never did get the credit due to him."

Laurence looked beyond Clarkson to Martin to see if this was some kind of inside joke thing or something, but Martin, having already been chastised once, averted his eyes down to his desk and the paperwork on it. The lieutenant turned his attention back to Clarkson. "I'm afraid you've lost me, Jim," he said. "Just what is it you're trying to say?"

"I'm saying that what we might have here is a Special Forces veteran. Someone who could lay their hands on one of these Goddamned super-fighting-knives, and more importantly, was trained in how to use it. You know, it can't be an easy thing to know exactly where to shove a knife through someone's ribs without the danger of killing them. There's also the gun—the little twenty-two. A Special Forces vet, someone who knows that biggest ain't always best, may well have chosen such a gun to suit the circumstances he knew he was gonna find himself in. .22 Long Rifle would be the ideal choice. Minimum noise, maximum effect at close-range—the classic round for a killer head shot."

"Jesus, Jim," Laurence said. "That Goddamn knife was made and probably issued back in 1941. If it was issued to our guy and he was maybe eighteen at the time, he'd be close to a fucking hundred by now!"

"I'm not saying that the knife was issued to him personally, just that he knew what it was capable of, how to use it properly, and where to get a hold of one."

Laurence threw his hands up in resignation. "Okay, so we—maybe—have ourselves a Special Forces vet as a contender for this. How does it help us?"

"Oh it mostly doesn't," Clarkson said. "I do like to speculate on what we'll finally rope in for this one, though. Besides, it's still a damn fine movie. You ought to rent it and give it a re-watch."

Chapter Six

He sat in the little café across from the small bar and watched the comings and goings. The place was an obvious biker haunt, that much was evident from the clientele that did come and go, and if the succession of obvious biker types entering and leaving the bar wasn't evidence enough to establish this, then the name of the place—The Hog Roost—should have been.

He was on his third cup of coffee and knew that, at his age, his bladder was not going to be able to take very much more.

It was his fourth day of "stakeout." The information he had gotten from Connor had been more or less verified on the very first day when the subject in question had rode up on a Harley and walked inside. The description matched the one that both Connor and the girl had given him. Besides, how many full-blooded Jicarilla Apache Indians could there be in residence in the city, who were also patrons of the bar that Connor had fingered?

From watching the place over the last few days, it had become obvious that the bar, or somebody in residence there, was dealing in more than bottles of Bud. A steady stream of unsavory-looking types were constantly entering the place only to exit again a very short time later.

The Indian himself was also fond of making regular appearances back outside to sit on the low brick wall that separated the bar from the parking garage of a small supermarket next door. While perched there, he would invariably make use of his cell phone. The watcher guessed that the reception inside the bar was none too good.

It had been a while now since the Indian had last been outside.

He looked at his watch—almost six. If the previous three days had been anything to go by, the guy should soon be making his final exit.

Sure enough, ten minutes later, the big Indian stepped outside with another biker-type alongside him. This guy was shorter, and nowhere near as well built as the Indian. He had long, straggly hair that may once have been able to be described as blond, which fell to the shoulders of his Colors jacket in greasy strings. He also sported a small, untidy goatee. The two men talked for a while before shaking hands, and the smaller guy strode off down the street while the Indian climbed atop his bike and roared off in the opposite direction.

He gave it a good fifteen minutes before leaving the café and walking across to the low brick wall opposite. He sat on the wall in the same place that the Indian usually sat when making or taking his calls, and reached behind him into the shrubbery that had been planted into the earthen embankment behind the wall. After a little delving, he found and retrieved the small recording device that he had installed there earlier that morning.

Chapter Seven

You could have found a near-identical wasteland in almost every big city across the USA. A brick and concrete desert, testimony to some structure or other that had once proudly graced the place, now littered with weeds, broken bricks, and other accumulated rubbish. The wind whistling in from the nearby river—the riverbanks every bit as bare and desolate as the wasteland itself was—only served to make the place feel even lonelier, sadder, and more forsaken.

The bulldozed, much-neglected area that sat awaiting the property developers and speculators' next master stroke was huge in area, and the nearest building—itself now a redundant, crumbling relic—was an abandoned multi-storey parking garage more than half a mile away from the center of the cleared space.

In its present condition, there was very little to recommend the site for use as anything. Nevertheless, despite all the drawbacks of isolation and remoteness, or rather *because* of them, it did have one thing in its favor. It was an ideal rendezvous for a drug deal.

Jimmy Wolf Eyes stepped from the passenger seat of the battered old Bronco pickup and surveyed the wide, open expanse of nothing that stretched in front of them. He left the Uzi on the seat behind him and walked around to the front of the pickup, signaling Mickey to cut the engine.

"You want me out there with you, Jimmy?" Mickey asked, poking his head through the open driver's window as he turned off the ignition.

"Just stay where you are," Jimmy told him. "And keep

that friggin' cut-down handy."

"Sure thing," Mickey said, reaching around to haul the Colt Commando into his lap. He pulled back and released the cocking lever, feeding a round into the chamber and making the weapon ready for action. "She's ready to rock, Jimmy," he called out. "Just let those motherfuckers start anything now!"

Jimmy sighed and put the heel of his palm to the side of his temple.

Christ, he felt like shit. He was using too much, he knew, and made himself a promise to cut back once this was all over. It wasn't easy not to use, though, given the shit that he'd been through the last few weeks. He wished he'd never gotten into the whole shitty mess of a deal in the first place. The heist and everything that had followed had been a total bummer from the word go, and now here he was, trying to make another major deal with nothing but Mickey for back-up. Mickey was okay, but he was no Connor when it came to handling a Diamondback or an Uzi. Not for the first time that day, he wished it were Connor sitting in the cab behind him. But Connor was 600 miles away in another Goddamn city, trying to sell his own fucking parcels. All thanks to that total fuck-up Farrell. Jesus, he had known from the first time he set eyes on the weasely little jacked-up fuck that he was going to be nothing but trouble.

Still, it was Farrell who had had the info, and who had set it all up. Somehow or other, the little weasel had gotten to know about a regular drug drop—ten to twelve kilos minimum—made by a small Cuban cartel on a deserted stretch of the Florida coast.

Even with Farrell involved, the heist had seemed like an easy enough operation, and the plan they had formulated was simple and workable—let the Cubans make the drop and then allow them to head back out to sea before moving in on the four local crackers who were there to make the pick-up.

It had seemed simple enough, and initially, it had been.

They had materialized out of the underbrush—himself, Connor, and Farrell—taking the four local rubes completely by surprise, and thanks to the show of force presented by the Colt Commando, Diamondback, and Uzi, had quickly convinced the men that it would be a wise decision to ditch their hardware. Then, with the lift almost complete and everything looking sweet, things had quickly begun to unravel.

He had been just about to approach the four crackers, the plastic cable ties already in his hand to serve as handcuffs, when that fucking Irish idiot had begun to cut loose, pumping round after round into the line of standing men. One of the men had started to make a run for it, and Connor had had no choice but to join in, bringing the man down before he could disappear into the undergrowth.

All four of the men were soon down on the ground, probably already dead, but the crazy little Irish prick had continued to pepper them with bullets, laughing like a maniac as he pumped round after round into the grounded men.

He was still firing when Jimmy had walked over to him and clubbed him upside the head with the butt of the Uzi.

He had come dangerously close to using the business end of the gun then, and it had only been Connor's intervention that had stopped him from shooting the crazy fucker.

That should have been warning enough to split the gear up right then and there and go their separate ways, but once again, Connor had talked him into sticking together and unloading all the dope in one deal as originally planned.

Against his better judgement, he had listened to Connor and to all the excuses he had made for Farrell. He wished now that he hadn't done so.

The little prick was a fucking bad luck owl of the first order, he was now convinced. After the snatch, things had gone from bad to worse. At the initial try of selling the stuff on, and then again later in Philly. Especially in Philly. Especially the incident with the little girl. Jesus, that fucking Farrell!

His thoughts were interrupted by the arrival of the other car, a big, black Cadillac Escalade.

Yeah, that's right, be inconspicuous why don'tcha? Jesus, the fuck-heads you have to deal with in this line of work.

"You believe this, Mickey?" he called out.

"Yeah, nice friggin' ride, Jimmy," Mickey responded with an edge of admiration in his voice. "Never mind, we'll maybe be able to drive around in one ourselves when this is done and dusted."

Jimmy gave a mental wince and repeated his last thought to himself.

Jesus, the fuck-heads you have to deal with.

The Caddy kept coming, rolling slowly toward them, and

then came to an easy, gravel-crunching halt about fifty yards away.

The driver's door opened and a guy stepped out who could have doubled as the sinister, second-rank heavy in any gangster film ever made. Tall and bald, built like an Abrams battle tank, and wearing the ubiquitous mirrored shades and black leather windbreaker.

Dear Lord, do all these clowns shop at the same friggin' store? Maybe there is a Mob Heavies 'R Us out there somewhere?

The guy came around to the front of the SUV and stood there with his hands folded in front of his dick.

Oh, you are fuckin' shittin' me! Jimmy thought.

"You bring the stuff?" the guy called out.

Jimmy gave a sigh of weariness at the sheer stupidity of the question.

He was tempted to shout back, "No, we thought we'd have a dress rehearsal first," but instead let it go and merely nodded his head.

The passenger door of the car opened up then and a second guy climbed out, this one a lot smaller and slimmer than the first guy and nicely suited up. He came around to the front of the Escalade and shouted across the distance between them. "I'm gonna send one of my guys over to pick up a test sample. You let him choose a package at random and then he'll bring it back here for testing, okay?"

"That's fine so long as he brings the money with him so's we can check that out too," Jimmy called back.

"That's not how it works," the suit sang out with an obvious edge of irritation to his voice.

"It is when I do a deal," Jimmy answered. "Your guy brings the money across so I can check it, then on his way back with the sample, he leaves the money smack in the middle. The shit tests out okay, your guy comes back over and picks up the rest of it. You all drive away, leaving the money in place, and that's it. Everybody happy, deal closed, pleasure doing business."

The suit glared back at him. "Mr. Redbone ain't gonna like it that you didn't trust him," he said.

"I can live with that. And you can tell Mr. Redbone that I woulda trusted him a lot more if he'd stuck to the script. We agreed on two people only."

"What, Max?" The suit gave a bark of laughter. "Hell, Max ain't muscle. He's just a friggin' chemist. Get on out here, Max."

One of the big car's rear doors opened up and a portly little guy in a rumpled suit climbed out.

"Take your jacket off, Max," the suit ordered.

Max did as he was told, carefully removing his suit jacket and placing it back into the car.

"Now give us a twirl."

The little fat guy put his arms in the air and did a slow, shuffling 360-degree turn.

"See, clean as a whistle," the suit declared. "Or would you like him to take the pants off too?"

"I don't give a fuck if he strips down to a hard-on," Jimmy snarled. "He's still a third party where there wasn't supposed to be one. He comes across here, he better come across carrying the money, otherwise I'm getting back in the truck and we're gone."

At this point, the big goon standing in front of the Escalade threw his hat into the ring.

"Mr. Howard, why don't you let me—"

"Shut the fuck up, Ed!" The suit bristled. "If I wanted Tonto here to know my friggin' name, I woulda sent him a fucking business card." He turned back to Max and barked out orders. "Get the money out the trunk. Take it across, let the fucker look at it, and then do like he says, put it down on the ground between us on the way back."

Two minutes later, Jimmy was looking into an open attaché case, riffling through the neatly stacked and banded bundles of currency. He smiled to himself, and some of the pressure he had felt building up at his temples and behind his eyes began to dissipate. The deal was on, and it looked like this one was going to go down smoothly.

Chapter Eight

Clarkson was sitting behind the tiny desk when Martin burst into the office clutching a small pile of folders to his chest. The young agent's excitement was obvious from the shine of his eyes.

"Boss, you're a friggin' genius!" he blurted.

"Well, this is something that I myself have always been aware of, but what brings you to the same conclusion?" Clarkson asked.

"You called it just right. That movie you mentioned, the one with Liam Neeson?"

Clarkson snapped his fingers. "That's the guy! I *knew* it would come to me."

Martin ignored him and carried on. "I ran that query on torture-killings through the database. You were right. We got a boatload of hits. Jeez, I never knew there were so many out-and-out sickos out there. So, in order to keep it manageable, I narrowed the search criteria to show only cases where electricity had been used in some way. I was thinking I'd maybe get back a dozen or so hits, but you'd be amazed. Jesus, there must have been—"

"Joseph, could we maybe cut to the chase here, son?" Clarkson said.

"Okay, well I'm working my way through these reports, and believe me, boss, they don't make for very nice reading."

Clarkson gave him the look, and Martin hurried on.

"So, bottom line is when I came across this particular one, it practically leapt off the page at me. Jesus, boss, it was just like you said, near identical to what happened in the movie. The victim tape-wrapped to a wooden chair and nails driven into his legs then wired up to the electrics."

"You're shittin' me!" Clarkson exclaimed, coming to attention now in his chair.

"Uh-uh." Martin shook his head in denial. "Just like in the Goddamn picture. The movie was called *Taken*, by the way.

"That's what I said," Clarkson answered with a puzzled frown.

Martin let it go.

"When was this?" Clarkson asked.

"That's the best bit. The killing took place just one week before our own. The guy wasn't shot, though. The killer just wrapped duct tape around his lower face until he couldn't breathe, and then left him there."

"Jeez!" Clarkson shuddered at the prospect. "I think I'd rather take the friggin' bullet. And where was this, Joseph?"

"Philadelphia. Same kind of scuzzy, low-rent rooming place that we found Connor in. The victim was another ex-con. Irish guy name of Farrell, Brendan Farrell. I'm getting his sheet wired through."

"You did good, Joseph," Clarkson said.

"Oh no wait, there's more." The young agent was positively beaming now. "We got quite a few hits on the knife—those things sell really well, over forty nation-wide over the last year or so. But guess what? One of them was sold less than a friggin' month ago by a militaria dealer in—"

"Beautiful downtown Philly!" Clarkson finished for him. "Pack your bags, Joseph. We are off to the city of brotherly love."

Chapter Nine

From his position way up in one of the upper stories of the abandoned parking garage, he had a really good view of the wasteland below, and the activity that was taking part slap in the middle of the urban desert.

The view through the rifle's scope brought that activity into much clearer focus.

He was lying atop the padded shooting mat he had brought with him, along with the rifle and all its accessories.

The weapon was a 7.62mm ex-military M21 of the Vietnam War era. It was the US military's designated marksman, or sniper, rifle of the time, being little more than a slightly customised M14 battle rifle with a scope and bipod added.

After a long trudge through the upper levels many hours before, he had found a near-perfect hide for himself, a place where part of the low exterior wall had crumbled away to provide a small opening through which he could look and fire.

He aligned the scope onto one of the two vehicles parked out in the wilderness—a large, black SUV—and did some fine tuning until the image became crystal clear. He panned the scope away from the vehicle to his right eastwards toward the river until he came to the small scrap of orange tape fastened to one of the many rusted steel reinforcing bars that sprang up from the jumble of concrete slabs. Although it looked innocuous enough, the small piece of tape that fluttered in the steady breeze coming in off the river was not there by accident. He had risked trekking across the concrete wasteland at first light in order to tie it in place. It was his wind indicator.

Satisfied that the wind had hardly changed since his last check, he swung the rifle back toward the waiting vehicles to the battered old pickup this time, and to the large, imposing figure of the Indian who stood before it.

The scope he was using employed mil dot markings on the

crosshair lines, and he began to put these to use now to accurately gauge the range. He put the horizontal cross hair directly in line with the top of the Indian's head, and counted down the mil dots to the bottom of his boots. It came out at 2.4.

Now he used the standard calculation of taking the size of the target in yards—he had seen the Indian fairly close up and put him to be six-four or thereabouts, which gave him 2.1 yards—and multiplying it by 1,000. This gave him 2,100. The final step in the formula was to divide this by the mil reading he had taken—2.4. This gave him a distance to the target of 875 yards. It was a long shot, and getting close to the rifle's maximum effective range, but he had every confidence in both the firearm and his own shooting ability.

Having established the range, he consulted the range card that he had painstakingly built up for the rifle and ammunition combination over the years. His ammunition was hand-loaded by himself to ensure maximum accuracy. He was using a Sierra .308 diameter Hollow Point Boat Tail, Match King bullet weighing 175 grains that, with the same carefully measured amount of propellant behind it, would consistently deliver a muzzle velocity of 2,600 feet per second.

The rifle was set to zero for 100 yards To compensate for bullet drop over longer distances, he would have to adjust the sight accordingly.

The card showed an elevation of 7.8 mil for 850 yards and 8.6 mil for 900. He split the difference and decided on a setting of 8.2, beginning to crank the elevation dial atop the scope counter-clockwise until he reached the desired setting.

He had already made adjustments to the scope's windage setting earlier based on what he calculated the wind strength and direction to be.

Now, he settled himself down into a comfortable shooting position and lowered his head to the stock again, finding the figure of the Indian in the scope once more, and centering the crosshairs into the middle of his upper chest. He began to regulate his breathing, taking up the first pressure on the trigger as he did so, and was only a second or two away from actually taking the shot when he heard the ominous double-click of a weapon being cocked immediately behind his left ear. The next instant, there was something cold and hard being pressed sharply into the back of his head.

Chapter Ten

The office that they had been given the loan of in Philadelphia was not quite as small as the one that Lieutenant Laurence had recently provided for them, but had been allocated to them with even less grace. This was mainly due to the fact that the Philadelphia PD did not see why a Federal Agency should be allowed to muddy the waters of what to them, since there was no established drug connection at their homicide, was a clear-cut case for the Philadelphia Homicide Division.

Nevertheless, a link—albeit a tenuous one—had been established between the two killings, and this was no longer just similarities in the two cases of the killer's M.O. Both Connor's and Farrell's full rap sheets had finally come through to Martin. It hadn't taken him too long to discover a link between the two men. Both had been incarcerated in the Southern New Mexico Correctional Facility just outside Las Cruces, both for minor drug-related offences. What made that fact more interesting was that they had been there at the same time. Martin had delved a little deeper, and discovered the cherry on the top of the cake—they had actually been cellmates together for a period of just over eight months.

The two agents were sitting at their own small desks—at least this room was big enough to accommodate two desks—with Clarkson busy on the telephone while Martin was tapping away at his laptop.

Clarkson finished his conversation and replaced the receiver with a smile on his face.

"They finally agreed," he told Martin, causing the young agent to raise his eyebrows in query.

"The apartment, we got permission to go back in."

It had not been easy. The crime was almost three weeks old and the apartment had ceased to be a crime scene two full weeks ago. There had been opposition from all quarters—the Philadelphia PD, the building's owners, and the apartment's new tenants. But Clarkson had managed to pull a few strings, and they had been given a two-hour slot to investigate that very afternoon.

It worried Clarkson that the initial investigation had found neither drugs nor money at the murder scene. If this thing was drug-related then, in his mind, they should have found one or the other.

Which left just three possibilities.

One—the killer had taken the drugs or the money with him when he left. If this was the case, though, and if it was the same killer responsible for both deaths, then why had he chosen to leave both money and drugs behind after the second murder?

Two—the first officers on scene had acquired the drugs or the money. This was not unheard of, Clarkson was sad to admit, but even in cases where it did happen, the officers were more likely to take a cut for themselves rather than the entire amount.

Three—the drugs or the money were still there.

Martin had already shut his laptop down and was shrugging into his jacket. He was reaching down for the car keys—along with the office, they had been given the loan of an unmarked police car for the duration—when Clarkson beat him to it and snatched them up.

"I'll drive," he said, and then by way of explanation, "We got a bit of a detour to make. I'm gonna drop in on an old friend from Philly Narcotics, see if he's in the mood to return a favor."

The stern-faced, middle-aged woman who opened up the apartment door to them did so with obvious reluctance, especially when she saw what was in the hallway behind Clarkson and Martin.

"Is that a dog?" she asked.

Clarkson gave a glance back to the German Shepherd and his handler behind him.

"No, ma'am, that's Officer O'Leary," he said, bending to

ruffle the dog's fur. "He's one of Philly's finest undercover cops, a master of disguise, as you can see."

The dog's handler was unable to stifle his laughter.

The woman, though, was not amused. "Super don't allow no dogs in the apartments," she replied, bridling at Clarkson's answer and giving him the look.

"The super ain't got no say in the matter, ma'am—Mrs. Keogh, is it? This is official police business. We can do it the easy way, be in and back out in an hour or two, or you can elect for the hard way. We re-classify the apartment as an official crime scene, and you and your family move out for the duration, which I'm telling you is likely to be weeks rather than days if I have anything to do with it." It was an outrageous bluff, but he had always been a good poker player, and the woman didn't pick up on it.

A minute later, all three men were in the apartment, and the dog—whose name was Buddy, not O'Leary—was being lead from room to room by his handler.

Though just as small and drab as the apartment that Connor had been resident in, this one was much—very much—cleaner, and a lot easier on the olfactory system.

The dog went happily about his work, tail wagging like a metronome as he sniffed eagerly into every corner and behind every piece of furniture.

Mrs. Keogh followed them throughout the apartment.

"He ain't gonna make a mess in here, is he?" she repeatedly asked.

Finally, the dog's handler had about enough and turned on her. "Ma'am, this dog is better house-trained than most people. He's less likely to take a dump in here than these two agents are!"

Clarkson turned to Martin. "Uh-oh, looks like your bad toilet habits have been discovered, Joseph."

Martin grinned and the woman gave a haughty sniff, showing once more that she was far from amused.

They went into the kitchen last, and straightaway the dog made a beeline for the little pantry in the far corner. He sniffed and pawed excitedly at the crack at the bottom of the door before letting out a string of barks.

"Good boy, Buddy!" His handler encouraged him, rubbing the ruff of fur at his collar.

Clarkson strode across the small room and yanked open

the pantry door.

Buddy gave an excited yelp and darted inside, sniffing and woofing as his paws scrabbled frantically over the red-tiled floor. There was a large paper sack of potatoes stored down there along with some plastic bags containing other vegetables. Buddy's handler dragged the dog back out and gave him a treat, handing out lavish praise as he did so.

Martin and Clarkson quickly stepped in and began to remove the bags of vegetables until the floor was clear.

Clarkson drew a small Gerber folder from his pocket and used the handle of the knife to tap onto the tiles. "There's a cavity," he finally said. "Right here in the middle." He tapped the tiles in a couple of different places to indicate the difference in the sound. He pulled out his mini-Maglite and shone the beam all over the pantry floor.

There, right at the back against the rear wall, a tiny sliver of rough, hempen cord, lying flush along the right-angle where the tiles met the wall. He reached in with the knife and pried it out of the recess it had been pushed into, revealing a length of cord some five inches long. He gave it a tug, and the entire tiled floor of the pantry began to rise—the tiles had been fixed to a single sheet of ply.

"Gotcha!" he whispered to himself, and then reached in and withdrew the tiled-over board. The board had been laid across ordinary wooden floorboards, a central section of which had been cut away to provide a hidey-hole. Clarkson reached inside and came back out with a brown paper grocery sack. He placed it on the floor beside him and opened it up. It was full of neatly banded banknotes.

"Bingo!" he cried. Behind him, Martin was grinning, ear-to-ear while the dog handler was busy feeding Buddy another treat and piling more praise on him.

"Sweet Jesus!" Mrs. Keogh sang out, the corners of her mouth turning downwards into a grimace. "Is all that money real?" she asked. Nobody bothered to answer her and she began to slowly shake her head. It was not too hard to guess that she was mulling over the fact that all of that money had been there for the taking since she and her family had moved in.

"Joseph, get onto the precinct house and get the captain over here," Clarkson instructed. "I want him present when this money is counted and signed in." He turned to the dog handler. "Son, I need you to stay here as a witness until the captain arrives, okay?"

The officer nodded.

Clarkson reached back into the hole and fished around, but there was nothing else there.

"No drugs then?" Martin asked.

"No, but I'm guessing they were there, and in enough of a quantity to leave their signature behind for our friend Buddy here." He turned to the panting animal, now sitting relaxed on his haunches, and gave him a few "good boys" of his own.

Chapter Eleven

"We ain't gonna go do anything silly now, are we?"

The gruff, somewhat muffled voice came from immediately behind him, and in emphasis, the cold, metallic object was shoved a little harder into the back of his head.

He carefully shook his head no, knowing that he had already done something very silly.

The earplugs. Force of habit. He'd slipped them in as soon as he got down on the mat ready to set the shot up. With them in place, a damn grizzly bear could have come waltzing up behind him without him noticing.

As if to underscore what he had been thinking, a set of calloused fingers were suddenly at the side of his head, closing in upon the protruding stub of bright orange plug embedded in his left ear and tugging it free.

"You hearing me okay?" the voice asked, a lot clearer now.

He gave a slight nod of his head in affirmation.

"Good. 'Cause I don't want there to be no misunderstanding between us. Any misunderstandings here are like to wind up with you feeling a mite lightheaded, that gonna be 'count of most of the inside of your head suddenly relocating itself to the outside. You get me?"

Again, the slight nod of the head.

"Now, first off, you needs to be uncurling that finger from where it's wrapped around the trigger there, only real slow and real easy like. Any sudden movements on your part is liable to cause that same lightheadedness, if you get my drift."

He did as he was told, releasing the pressure he had already built up upon the trigger and letting it ease back into position before removing his finger from the trigger-guard and resting it alongside the stock.

"That be good," the voice behind him said. "I can see you

gonna be real sensible about this."

He felt the pressure of the hard, cold metal being removed from the back of his head.

"Hell, I still cain't believe I done found you up here," the voice came again. "Boss done told me to check it out just in case. Though I have to admit, I never thoughts to find anything. Guess that's why he the boss, huh? Say, man, you don't really think you coulda made that shot, do you?" he asked. "Hell, they gots to be half a damn mile away."

He smiled to himself. The guy behind him had a good sense of distance if nothing else. He softly answered, "It isn't that hard."

"The hell you say!" the voice replied. "Now, the next thing I want you to do is to crawl back aways from the piece and then *slowly* stand up."

That was a mistake. He should have left him where he was and simply made him roll away from the rifle and onto his back. A man lying flat on his back had very little attack options open to him.

He rose to all fours and began to move away from the rifle in a reverse crawling motion.

"Okay, that's far enough. Now stand up, and don't be forgetting the slow part."

"It's not likely to be anything *but* slow, mister," he said, turning his head to look at the man behind him for the first time. As expected, the guy was tall, stocky, and black. He held a large stainless revolver pointing straight at his face. "I got a bum knee," he said by way of further explanation. He looked directly at the big, shiny revolver the guy was holding so nonchalantly, recognizing it as a Colt Python .357 magnum. "Hell, I didn't think any of you gangsta types went in for wheelguns anymore."

If the black guy took any exception to the "gangsta" reference, he didn't show it. He glanced at his gun and shrugged. "I always found 'em more reliable," he said. "Less to go wrong, no safety catches to be fumbling with or overstressed mag springs to worry about." All of which was perfectly true. "Besides, this thing will stop a Goddamn elephant in its tracks." That last bit most certainly wasn't.

Not for the first time, he found himself wondering how such a mediocre cartridge—little better than a souped-up .38—had attained such a near-mythical reputation.

"Jeez, Pop, ain't you a little old for this kind of stuff?" the black man asked, getting his first good look at the shooter's face.

"Son, I was a little old for this kind of stuff when I was in my prime," he answered, and then began to laboriously climb to his feet. He pulled his left leg up until his foot was flat upon the concrete below, and then used it to help lever himself up. He gave a grunt of pain as his knee popped in complaint, and he put out his left hand to grab hold of it to steady himself.

The small movement caused the black man to focus his attention on the shooter's left hand. He didn't see what the right hand—now shielded by the shooter's body—was doing. Not until it was too late anyway.

With a sudden upwards lunge, the shooter was rising to his feet and turning around to confront him, moving with a speed that belied his obvious age. There was something small and silver clutched in the guy's right hand, a hand that was whipping up and around to point directly into his face. He was still bringing the Python up to line it back up with the shooter's head when whatever was in the shooter's hand erupted in a little fireball of flame.

No sooner had he identified it for what it was, when something slammed into his eye with incredible force, setting of lightning bolts of dazzling brilliance inside his head.

He was dimly aware of the deafening roar of the .357 going off in his hand, and was halfway through thinking how badly his reputation was going to suffer—letting a senile old fart get the better of him—when everything went into total blackout with the swiftness and surety of an electric light being turned off.

Chapter Twelve

The sign above the shop's façade read SS Vintage Arms & Collectable Militaria. The writing was flanked on either side by a set of crossed flags—the national flags of the USA and the UK.

"What's with the Limey flag, do you think?" Clarkson asked.

"Beats me," Martin replied, stooping down to look at some of the items on display in the window. "Given the name of the place and the nature of some of these items, I would have thought a swastika would have been more in keeping."

"Swastika ain't a flag, Joseph, it's a symbol, and one that's a lot older than the Goddamn German Nazi party."

He too bent to look into the window. Once he did, he had to concur with the young DEA agent. There did seem to be an abundance of Nazi related articles behind the glass, a good proportion of which were indeed adorned with the infamous swastika emblem.

They went inside, their entrance being heralded by a tiny brass bell above the door. The interior was large and spacious and well laid-out, most of the items for sale residing inside tasteful wooden and glass display cabinets. The majority of the cases contained collectable militaria in the form of medals, edged weapons, uniform insignia etc., but some of the cases contained firearms—both long guns and handguns, and there were more firearms mounted as display pieces on most of the walls.

In addition, there were quite a few basic, human figure mannequins scattered throughout the floorspace and decked out in a variety of military uniforms.

The tinkling of the bell had brought an elderly assistant out from the back office, and he approached them now with an easy smile upon his face. He was tall and slim, and appeared to be decidedly overdressed for the role of sales assistant, wearing a stylish, if somewhat old fashioned, navy blue pinstripe over a crisp white shirt. His tie was dark blue to match the suit, and covered with a pattern of small red bars. As he came closer, Clarkson could see that the small red bars were actually representations of boats.

"Can I help you gentlemen?" he asked.

"Well, we certainly hope so, Mr....?" Clarkson said.

"Stevens, Geoffrey Stevens," the old guy answered, extending his hand.

Clarkson took it and gave it a pump. "James Clarkson, I'm a Federal Agent, sir." He had long since given up using the CADI initials—hardly anyone was aware of what they even stood for. "And this is my assistant, Joseph Martin."

"Pleased to meet you, Mr. Clarkson, you too, Mr. Martin," Stevens said, transferring his handshake to the younger man.

"Now, how may I be of help?"

"Are you the proprietor, Mr. Stevens?" Clarkson asked.

"Oh no, that would be my brother, my younger brother, Sean," Stevens replied. "Hence the name SS—Sean Stevens. Although, I do help him run the place."

"We really would like to speak with the proprietor, if that's okay?"

"I'm afraid that won't be possible, Mr. Clarkson. My brother isn't here at the moment. What did you say this was concerning?"

"We didn't, sir. Is it possible to contact your brother, have him drive over for an interview? It really won't take very long."

"I'm afraid you misunderstand me, Mr. Clarkson. When I say my brother isn't here, I don't mean he isn't in the shop. He isn't in the city. He has had to go away on business."

"Oh, where to?" Clarkson asked.

"Why, I really don't know. Out of town was all he said."

"Well, couldn't you call him? Find out?"

"Call him?" Stevens' face showed a look of true puzzlement.

"Sure, on his cell phone, you know?"

Stevens burst out laughing, and then stopped when he saw the look on Clarkson's face. "I'm so sorry, Mr. Clarkson, but just the thought of Sean carrying a cell phone with him. Well, it's certainly an amusing prospect to say the least. I'm afraid he has a deeply rooted hatred of the blasted things, as indeed, I must confess, I myself do. I guess it's an age thing. My brother is only three years younger than myself."

Clarkson sighed. "Mr. Stevens, I take it that neither you nor your brother were born in the US?"

"Oh Good Lord no!" Stevens exclaimed, and then as an afterthought. "Oh, no offense meant, naturally."

"None taken, naturally," Clarkson answered. "British, is it?"

"Ah, you're too good, sir. You have it in one. Just what was it that gave me away?"

"Well, I guess mostly it was *Salem's Lot*."

"Beg pardon, sir?"

"You know, the vampire movie. Forget True Twilight, or whatever it's called. *Salem's Lot*—friggin' scariest vampire movie I ever saw. James what's-his-name. The antique shop owner. Man, if they ever do another re-make, you should hustle along to the auditions." Behind him, he could hear the soft chuckles coming from Martin. In front, all he was getting from Stevens were blank, confused stares.

"Okay," Clarkson said, "if Mr. Stevens—the other Mr. Stevens, I mean—isn't here, perhaps you *can* help us after all. We are trying to track down the buyer of a knife that we believe may have been bought from this store. Joseph?" He turned around to attract the young agent's attention. Martin was heavily engrossed in the contents of a nearby display case.

"Sir?" he asked.

"The photographs, Joseph? The knife?"

"Oh, yes, of course." He came over to the counter, withdrawing the photos as he did so and placing them atop the glass top.

"Sir, we have been informed that you sold one of these quite recently?"

"Ah, a Fairbairn-Sykes, and from the looks, a rather splendid early edition one at that. Why yes, I remember the official query we had now. Really, Mr. Clarkson, if that was all you wanted to verify, you should have said so from the beginning." Stevens sounded slightly piqued.

"Sir, do you think that the knife in the photographs might

be the same as the one that you sold?"

Stevens stepped away to the side and opened up one of the drawers built into the far side of the display cabinets. He returned with a large magnifying glass. He then bent to the photographs with the glass held out in front of him, making little mutterings and comments to himself as he did so.

Finally, he replaced the glass onto the countertop and addressed the two agents.

"Well, normally, it's hard to be absolutely sure. I mean, these things weren't allocated serial numbers the way firearms would be, but yes, everything does seem to point to it. The S-shape of the hand guard, the fine knurling on the handle, and the unusual squared-off area—or ricasso—at the bottom of the blade, coupled with the markings that are etched there. On the obverse, we have Fairbairn and Sykes' own design mark." Here, he paused to place a finger on the squared off tablet area just ahead of the knife's hand guard on one of the photographs.

The legend etched into the metal could still be easily read—THE F-S FIGHTING KNIFE.

"And here on the reverse." He switched his finger to the other photograph, showing the other side of the knife's blade, and pointed to the same area. Here, the acid-etched area read—WILKINSON SWORD Co. Ltd. LONDON with the firm's famous crossed-sword logo overlaying the writing. "This is the more important of the two markings," Stevens told them. "There have been some excellent reproductions of the early pattern knives, most notably the ones done by The Castle Knife Company back in the 1970s, and more recently, the fine ones turned out by Macdonald Armouries of Edinburgh. Both companies, though, have the reverse ricasso etched with their own company legends in order to prevent them from being passed off as originals. As I said, it normally would be very difficult to tell one early pattern F-S from another, if they were both in a similar condition. However, with this particular knife, there is no question that it is the same one that we bought and sold."

"And how can you be so sure?" Clarkson could feel his pulse beginning to quicken as he asked the question.

Stevens took hold of one of the photographs and, turning it around, placed it closer to the two agents. "Can you see the markings here on the hand guard?" He pointed to a series of small, vertical grooves that had been cut or filed into the metal of the cross piece.

"What, they're not part of the original design?" Clarkson asked.

"Oh indeed not, sir. They are the reason that I remember the knife so distinctly. You see, I handled the original purchase of the knife, and I can remember the gentleman in question telling me, in rather dramatic fashion, that they were 'kill marks'—something akin to the 'notches' that some of your Wild West gunfighters were said to be prone to cutting into the butts of their pistols."

Clarkson leaned down for a closer look. The small, evenly spaced cuts that he had at first taken to be jimping grooves similar to those let into the spine of his folder were spaced centrally across the hand guard and numbered six in total.

"So, we're saying that whoever originally owned this thing made six kills with it?"

"Either that or whoever wanted to pass the piece on did it themselves to lend an aura of mystique to the weapon, and possibly a few extra dollars to its value." Stevens was smiling now. "Whatever the real story of those notches is, they instil in me no hesitation in declaring that this is indeed the very knife that was bought by my good self, and then sold on at a later date." He handed the photographs back to Clarkson.

"And do you keep records as to who would have purchased it?"

"Why of course we keep records." Stevens seemed positively affronted at the question.

"Do you think then, Mr. Stevens, that you could access those records and tell us who actually made the purchase?"

"Well of course I can," Stevens replied, and Clarkson felt his pulse shift into an even higher gear.

"If you will just excuse me a moment, gentlemen?" Stevens said. With that, he made a brief sortie into the back office, and was back a minute or two later carrying a large accounts ledger. "Now then, let me see," he said, withdrawing a pair of elegant, gold-framed, half-moon spectacles from his outer breast pocket and placing them atop his nose. He began flipping back through the pages of the ledger, stopping at certain pages as he did so and running his finger down the columns of listed items.

Clarkson began tapping the glass counter in obvious frustration, but Stevens either didn't pick up on the signals given off, or simply chose to ignore them.

"Ah yes, here we are!" he finally declared, and Clarkson was sorely tempted to reach out and snatch the book from him. His better judgement prevailed, though, and he waited for Stevens to reveal what he had found. "Yes, I thought as much. It was my brother who actually conducted the sale. I didn't think I'd disremember actually selling the item myself."

Disremember? Clarkson thought. *Is there actually such a friggin' word?*

"Who was the buyer?" Clarkson asked, gesturing for Martin to come across and take down the details.

"That would be a Mr. Stirling, sir. A Mr. D. Stirling."

"Good man," Clarkson said. "And the address?"

"Oh, I'm afraid there isn't one, sir. You see, we're not legally obliged to take down even a name for general militaria sales such as this. But my brother is rather pedantic on such matters, and does insist that we do. I'm afraid that the name is all we have to go on."

"No, not if he paid by plastic, we don't," Clarkson said. "If he paid by credit card, you can browse the transaction and come up with the card details, right?"

"Oh indeed we can, sir, but unfortunately, this was a cash transaction."

Clarkson let out a low moan and actually had his head in his hands when Martin came over to the counter.

"Mr. Stevens?" the younger agent said.

"Yes?"

"I'm just a little curious here. I see that a lot of your stock is tied into German World War Two stuff. And, in fact, to the Nazi party and the Waffen SS Divisions in particular?"

"It is indeed, sir," Stevens replied.

"Well, is there a specific reason for that?"

"A reason, sir?"

"Sure, you know, like do you or your brother have any political leanings that way?"

Stevens gave him a long and very intense look before finally electing to answer. "I take it—Mr. Marvin, was it?"

Martin chose to let it pass.

"That you are asking whether my brother or I have sympathies for, or connections to, the myriad number of Neo-Nazi organizations that your government has allowed to flourish in this wonderful land of the free that you have established here? You are quite correct in what you say, sir. A lot of our stock does relate to the German World War Two era, and as you rightly point out, to the Nazi party in particular. And do you know why that is so, Mr. Government Agent?" Stevens didn't even pause to let Martin reply. "It is, quite frankly, because that shit sells like hot cakes over here. Your patriotic, flag-waving, stand-up-and-be-counted die-hard Americans just can't seem to get enough of it. So, in answer to your question, no, neither I nor my brother has any political leanings that way. And before you leave, sir, and I would advise you to do so directly, I would like to ask *you* a question."

Martin, looking somewhat abashed by the old British guy's tirade, raised both his eyebrows and his hands as if to say, "fire away."

"Why don't you, sir, go and take a flying fuck at a rolling donut?"

Ten minutes later, in a nearby Starbucks, both agents were seated in a booth and nursing a coffee.

"Congratulations, Joseph," Clarkson finally said, "you just managed to turn Bruce Wayne's loveable English butler into Archie friggin' Bunker without even trying."

Martin said nothing, just continued to sit there, stirring and staring into his coffee cup.

"Something you want to tell me?" Clarkson finally asked.

"I ought to introduce you to my grandma one of these days," Martin said, finally lifting his head up to look at his boss. "You'd like her, I think—got lots of interesting stories to tell about the old days and the old country—Poland that was. You know, my grandma sure is an interesting old lady. Done a lot of interesting things in her time. Got herself a tattoo way, way before they became fashionable—hell nowadays, they're practically de rigueur. Only Grandma's isn't a cute little butterfly, or her name spelled in fuckin' Sanskrit or whatever. It's just numbers, just a long set of boring numbers, inked on forever, right here." He jabbed a finger at the inside of his left forearm.

For once, Clarkson was at a loss for words.

"What's the matter, boss? You got no movie hits to offer?" Martin's voice was raised now. "How about a quote from *Sophie's Choice* or maybe *Schindler's* fuckin' *List*?"

"Easy son," Clarkson advised, reaching over to place a hand on Martin's arm. "You're scaring the customers, and in a Starbucks, that'll probably get you a hamburger in Frackville."

Martin gave a rueful smile before running the fingers of his right hand through his hair. "I'm sorry, boss. It's just seeing all that shit in there—fucking swastikas everywhere. Christ, how can anyone make a living selling that stuff knowing what it stood for and all?"

"Well, like the feller said, Joseph, he couldn't if people weren't willing to buy it, and people obviously are. Hell, did you see the price tags on some of that stuff?"

"Jesus, boss, that's just like saying it's okay to sell crack cocaine based on the fact that the Goddamn dope heads are queuing up to buy the fucking shit!"

"Except for one small detail, Joseph. Selling crack is illegal, selling Nazi memorabilia is not. Maybe Mr. Stevens was right, maybe it's our fault, maybe we ought to make all that shit illegal too. But we don't, and there's a reason we don't. It's all about giving people the freedom of speech and freedom of expression. Freedom to choose their own brand of politics and beliefs, and that's what sets us apart from states like Hitler's Germany. So we don't make selling, buying, or owning any of that shit illegal, and until we do, there ain't a thing we can do about it. It just doesn't pay to worry about all the stuff we can't change, son. I learned that a *long* time ago."

"Maybe so," Martin said, "but I still intend to run both of those Limey fuckers through the system. There's something definitely pinging my radar about that pinstripe-wearing prick."

Chapter Thirteen

The first faint pop that Jimmy heard way off in the distance may or may not have been gunfire. The second deep, resonating boom that followed almost immediately most definitely was.

He looked out across the wasteland to where he thought the shot had come from. There was nothing to be seen there except the crumbling edifice of the old multi-storey. He quickly turned his attention back to his front.

The little chemist guy with the sample package of product had covered more than half the distance back to his own car after lying the money case down halfway between the vehicles, and had now stopped dead in his tracks, not knowing what the shot signified or what to do next.

Behind him the muscle-guy, Ed, was already reaching inside his windbreaker. Jimmy doubted if it was for a pack of smokes or gum.

Fuck!

He was reaching for his own piece when he heard the staccato harsh cracks of the Colt Commando opening up from behind.

Way to go, Mickey! he thought, and then immediately turned the praise into a litany of curses as he saw the little fat guy in front of him being tossed around like a rag doll.

That stupid greaseball, pothead Mickey had opened up on the fucking chemist!

Knowing that he likely had two armed assailants directly in front of him, Jimmy made a wise snap-decision. He turned around and ran, pulling the Hi-Power free from his belt as he did so.

For a split second, he contemplated ducking behind the Bronco's open passenger door and using that for cover while he retrieved the Uzi from the passenger seat. He decided against it, though, and kept going until he reached the back of the vehicle, hearing two very loud booms from the rear as he threw himself behind the tailgate.

He ducked down low behind the rear wheel and risked a quick peek out to the side. He was glad that he hadn't used the vehicle's door as a barricade—it just didn't cut the mustard as one, and was now sporting two large, ragged holes in the interior trim, through which he could see daylight on the far side.

Jesus, what was that big, bald fucker carrying?

He was about to yell out to Mickey to check if he was okay and get him to open up with the Commando, when he felt the truck shudder against his shoulder and the exhaust pipe began to belch fumes as the motor roared into life.

The next instant, the Bronco was on the move, heading away from him and veering off to his left.

Oh that fucking Mickey! He cursed as the cover of the truck was whipped away from him, leaving him totally exposed. In front of him, the squat bulk of the Cadillac lay just fifty yards distant. Of the gunman named Ed and the guy in the suit, there was no sign. They too must have taken the precaution of sheltering behind the cover of their own vehicle.

Jimmy knew that they would not remain hidden for long, though, once they realized what was happening and that they had a prime target totally devoid of cover.

With another tirade of curses directed at Mickey, he began to sprint after the revving Bronco, his eyes staying glued to the Escalade as he did so. He quickly caught up to the rear of the retreating vehicle and flung his pistol into the cargo bed, then gripped the top of the tailgate with both hands. He managed to get a booted foot onto the top of the rear bumper and haul himself up, his other foot reaching for and finally finding the same slippery surface.

For a few brief seconds, he crouched there, holding on to the tailgate and balanced on the bumper like a Roman charioteer on a desperate race around the Hippodrome. Then he saw the two figures stepping away from the rear of the Escalade, each man with both hands raised in front and pointed directly at him.

Shit!

He pulled forward with both hands, hauling himself over

the tailgate and tumbling head-over-heels into the bed of the truck. Off to his right, the handguns began to boom and crack.

There were a couple of metallic clangs, one decidedly louder than the other, as the bullets whacked against the pickup's side panel, and Jimmy was horrified to see a large tear open up in the metal of the panel as one of the slugs tore effortlessly through it, then just as easily ripped another hole through the pickup's far side.

Jesus, what is *that fucker using?*

Whatever it was, it was painfully obvious that the bed of the pickup was no safe refuge, no matter how low down he stayed.

He scrambled around frantically, looking for and locating the Hi-Power, and then popped his head and shoulders over the low side panel to return fire.

He squeezed off four or five quick shots in the general direction of the Escalade, knowing as he did so that he had very little chance of hitting anything—the truck was yawing and bouncing over the rough terrain like a Goddamn space-hopper.

Still letting rip with the Browning, he saw the big, bald guy take slow, deliberate aim—even from this distance the pistol huge in his hands—and felt his stomach clench into a tight ball of dread.

Then, incredibly, the guy's head just seemed to explode in a welter of red liquid.

Holy shit! Talk about a lucky fuckin' shot!

He stopped firing and began to switch his aim to the guy in the suit who was standing a good ten yards away from the head-shot big guy, and still popping away at him, probably with a nine from the sound of it. He was just trying to line up a bead when the suit's head went exactly the same way as the muscle guy's had, exploding into the atmosphere like an overripe watermelon.

Oh Sweet Jesus, it hadn't been one of his shots that had taken out the first guy. There was somebody else out there! Somebody holed up in that damn multi-storey, and that prize fuckup Mickey was heading directly for them.

He crawled his way to the front of the pickup's bed and began to use the butt of the Browning to hammer onto the rear window of the cab, yelling out for Mickey to veer away.

This time, he actually heard the far-off crack of the rifle, followed a second later by the crunching-ice sound that the bullet made as it slammed into and through the Bronco's windscreen.

The grimy rear window that he had been hammering on suddenly looked as though somebody had just thrown a bucket of red paint over it from the inside of the cab, and then the pickup began to lose speed and revs as the pressure was removed from the accelerator.

Oh Christ on a donkey, what a five-star fuckup!

Chapter Fourteen

Unusually, Clarkson was sitting at the desktop computer they had been provided with when Martin came into the office. Once again, the young agent was clutching a slim manila folder to his chest.

"Got the query back on those two Limeys," he told him.

"And?" Clarkson asked.

"Don't know yet, ain't had time to read through it all."

"But I'm guessing that neither one has a record, right?" Clarkson smiled.

"Not having a record don't mean a person ain't hinky, just means they ain't been *caught* being hinky," Martin retorted. "We'll see whether that place deserves another visit after I get through reading this."

"Oh the Stevens' boys are definitely due another visit, no matter what you find in that report."

"Yeah? Why is that?"

"While you were giving the shop's stock the once-over, I was more interested in the guy himself," Clarkson said. "You notice his tie?"

"Tie?"

"Yeah, you know, that thing you wear around your neck to keep your top shirt button done up."

Martin shrugged and shook his head, and Clarkson beckoned him over to the computer's monitor screen. There, smack in the middle, was an enlarged image of the same necktie that Geoffrey Stevens had been wearing—a dark blue background with small red boat silhouettes imprinted on it.

"Know what that is?" Clarkson asked. Again, Martin shook his head. "That, my boy, is the official necktie of the Special Boat Service."

"The what?" Martin asked.

"SBS. Special Boat Service. The British equivalent of our own Navy SEALs, only formed a good while earlier, way back in 1940, in fact, as the Special Boat Section. They were one of the original bad-ass Special Forces units, issued with and trained to use, among a whole host of other nasty weapons and devices, the Fairbairn-Sykes fighting knife. Also, I've been doing a little bit of knife research myself. You were absolutely right, Joseph, when you said those things were highly collectable and, in the right condition, generate a few bucks to say the least. I've been looking up some recent sales where first pattern Fairbairn-Sykes have been weighing in at over a grand. Which begs me to wonder why our mysterious Mr. Sean Stevens let one go for the less than princely sum of two hundred bucks."

This was interesting news indeed, and Clarkson was well pleased with himself for discovering it. It was not nearly so interesting, though, as the information that Martin discovered just an hour or two later and that sent him scurrying throughout the building in search of his boss.

Chapter Fifteen

He watched the big man stumble backwards with his eyeball blown clear out of its socket. The tiny .22 bullet had gone exactly where he had been aiming, clean through the guy's left eyeball.

The guy's magnum, on the other hand, had gone off harmlessly out into the windswept atmosphere beyond the low parapet as the black man had been reeling away from him.

He had been lucky, he knew, as he watched the man's legs buckle beneath him and his body began its swift descent to the hard concrete floor.

Lucky in that the man had been stupidly overconfident, the more so when he had seen his age, and then made some very wrong—and for him very dangerous—assumptions as to his abilities based upon his appearance.

He heard the sickening crunch as the back of the man's head made violent contact with the concrete below, and stepped a little closer to make sure of the guy's condition.

It only took a second or two to satisfy himself that the guy was not coming back up for the count, no matter how long that count might be.

He shoved the tiny .22 back into the pocket of his cargo pants and made his way quickly over to the rifle.

As he had already guessed from the distinctive sounds of what seemed like a distant firework display, things had gone into cluster-fuck mode down below.

He hunkered down and got his eye to the scope. The pickup truck was on the move and headed directly toward him. He had a fleeting glimpse of his quarry perched on the back of the vehicle, and then rolling himself into the cargo area to disappear behind the pickup's cab. He panned the rifle and scope to the left, coming to a halt when he reached the big, black SUV and the two armed figures that had now emerged from behind it.

They were both standing in the classic, two-handed, Weaver-grip firing position, and both aiming toward the pickup as it made its slow, lumbering way across the debris-strewn ground.

No! he thought. The Indian was his. He had made a promise, and he'd be damned if these two coke-dealing motherfuckers were going to make him break it.

He took quick aim at the big, bald guy who appeared to be firing some kind of hand-held cannon—the report and muzzle-flash were impressive even at this distance. He took just a moment to steady his breathing, and squeezed off the shot. He didn't wait to confirm the hit, but was already swinging the scope onto the other guy before the rifle had even fully recovered from the recoil of the first round.

Again, a fraction of a second to regulate his breathing, and then that same gentle squeeze of the trigger. This time, he held on the target, watching impassively as the guy's head disintegrated in a red-tinted cloud of blood, bone fragments, and brain tissue.

He swung back onto the approaching pickup then and did a quick calculation as to how much nearer the truck now was to his firing position. Not having the time to make the necessary scope adjustments, he simply aimed off, using the mil dot above the crosshairs for his aiming point. He centred in on the middle of the windscreen on the driver's side and squeezed off another round. The windscreen shattered and the vehicle began to slow. It continued to roll forward before finally coming to a complete halt, and he settled in to await the appearance of the Indian.

Even though he was expecting it, he had to admit when the guy did reappear, he was incredibly quick. He was up and over the tailgate in one agile bound and then sprinting off toward the other vehicle in an unpredictable series of zigs and zags. Jesus, the guy would have made a good pro football player.

He decided to go for the ambush technique rather than attempting to shoot him on the run and swung the scope to focus on the area directly in front of the black SUV, waiting for his target to run into his sights.

He lifted his eye a fraction from the rubber eyepiece to

see just how far away the Indian was, and was surprised to find he had made a detour, jinking back out away from the SUV toward where the pickup had been parked earlier. Was the guy seriously thinking about leaving the vehicle behind and making it away on foot? His curiosity got the better of him and he swung the scope back onto the zig-zagging figure. It all made sense when he saw him stoop without actually stopping to snatch up the aluminium case that was lying on the ground. With the case in hand, he began to jink his way back to the car.

He decided to try and get him on the run, giving him a slight lead and trying to anticipate his next sideways twist. He called it right and the Indian veered toward his crosshairs. He pulled the trigger, only to swear in frustration as he saw him twist away again at the last second. The bullet missed him by inches, kicking up shards of concrete as it slammed into the ground. He quickly adjusted his aim and fired again, or tried to. The rifle had jammed.

Chapter Sixteen

When Martin finally caught up with his boss, it was in another Starbucks, this one just a block away from the precinct house.

Clarkson could see that the agent was excited. He took a last pull on his coffee and pushed a half-eaten Danish away from himself. "You want coffee?" he asked.

"Hell no!" Martin replied. "I got something, boss. Something that could connect an awful lot of friggin' dots."

"Okay, so shoot," Clarkson said.

"Well, the guy that we spoke to—Geoffrey—we drew a blank there. Nothing, not even a Goddamn parking ticket. But his brother, again nothing criminal, but get this—twelve years ago he's involved in a bad auto wreck on the freeway, apparently swerved to avoid some drunken lunkhead coming from the opposite direction who had crossed the divider. Anyway, the vehicle he's travelling in does a very impressive roll and tumble, bouncing down the highway head-over-heels before finally coming to rest upside down with our Mr. Stevens still strapped firmly and snugly into the driver's seat. The only thing is, Mr. Stevens is now unconscious, and the car begins to catch alight. By this time, quite a few cars have pulled up in close proximity, but all that most of these mothers can think to do is stand back and gawk. Hell, some of them even pull out their cells and begin doing a photo-shoot of the whole damn thing. Except for one person, that is. This tiny little Vietnamese guy—Tran Than Chinh, owns a Mom and Pop grocery store back in Philly—he gets out of his own car and runs across to help. Bear in mind that by this time, the vehicle is starting to really light up the highway; also bear in mind that this little Asian guy must weigh all of one hundred and fifteen pounds fully dressed and sopping wet.

Anyway, he does no more than climb into the cab, cuts our unconscious Limey out of his seat harnesss, and then drags him back out to safety just seconds before the whole damn thing erupts like a friggin' Roman Candle."

"And this ties in to our investigation how?" Clarkson asked.

"Well, it doesn't, or rather didn't. Not until a month or so ago when a little Vietnamese girl was dragged off the street, brutally gang-raped, and left for dead. I'm betting you can probably guess whose daughter she is."

Clarkson said nothing, and Martin continued.

"That ain't all. I pulled the crime sheet for the rape. The homicide cops had a local sex and drug offender that they really liked for it, and were doing their best to locate him for questioning, when guess what?"

"Somebody beat them to it," Clarkson said, his voice soft and low. "Somebody who questioned our Mr. Farrell a lot harder than they ever could."

If Martin was disappointed that Clarkson had stolen his punch line, he didn't show it. He sat back, watching him run things together in his head. "So, what do you think, boss?" he finally asked.

"I think we need to pay another visit to that friggin' shop, find out just where the other Mr. Stevens is currently at. I'm also wondering just how in hell do you ever repay a guy who saves you from being toasted alive like a marshmallow?"

Clarkson had been tempted to ask Martin to remain in the car when they made their second visit to SS Vintage Arms. He knew, though, that the young agent would consider this a great affront to his dignity, and made do with a quiet word of caution before they entered.

Geoffrey Stevens was busy with a customer when they first entered, although the little tinkling bell had warned him of their arrival. He glanced in their direction as they came in, his look cold and frosty as he recognized them, and then turned back to the customer, all sweetness and light.

They waited until the guy had made his purchase and left the shop before approaching Stevens.

Before Stevens could say anything, Clarkson held up his hand in a placatory gesture. "Mr. Stevens, we're not here to cause you any trouble or cast any more aspersions on the type of merchandise you're selling here," Clarkson said.

Stevens looked at Martin, and the young agent gave him what he hoped would be taken as a smile of apology.

Clarkson continued. "We do need your help in what is a very serious matter, however. Your help and your full cooperation."

"I take it this involves the Fairbairn-Sykes?" Stevens said.

Clarkson nodded. "The knife and some other things, yes."

"Am I to assume that the knife was recently used in a crime then?" Stevens asked.

"I'm afraid so," Clarkson said, and then came directly to the point. "Mr. Stevens, is it true that you were once a member of the Special Boat Service?"

The old guy gave a faint, barely noticeable smile. "You are to be commended upon your knowledge of military neckwear, agent Clarkson."

"And was your brother also a member of the SBS?"

Stevens looked slightly shocked and taken aback. "Sean? Good Lord, no! Sean's military career began and ended with a two-year stint in his grammar school's Army Cadet Force. Although, given his ability as a marksman, perhaps it should have been Sean and not myself who made a career of the military."

"Marksman?" Clarkson asked.

"Oh yes indeed," Stevens confirmed. "My brother is a fine rifle shot, agent. A natural talent that he discovered when he was in the cadets."

Clarkson didn't know what to make of that. Both of the two murders had been committed up close, and very personal, so to speak.

"The fact is, Mr. Stevens, we really do need to contact your brother," he told the elderly assistant. "It is absolutely vital that we talk to him as soon as possible."

"As I think I've already told you gentlemen, until Sean returns, I have no way *of* contacting him," Stevens said.

"You mean he hasn't been in touch at all since he left?" Clarkson asked.

"No, I'm afraid he hasn't."

"And just when was that?"

Before answering, Stevens took out a small pocket diary and consulted it. "Let me see," he said, flipping back the pages as he spoke. "That would have been the thirtieth, which is what, nine days ago?"

"Isn't that an unusually long time for a business trip, Mr. Stevens?"

"Not really. My brother will always take time out to visit local arms fairs and other dealers whenever he's out of town, or even take the opportunity to enter a competition or two, depending on where he finds himself."

"Competition?" Clarkson asked.

"Yes," Stevens responded, and Clarkson could tell that this was an area that he was not too fond of discussing. He waited for the shop assistant to elaborate. "I'm afraid my brother has a rather unusual hobby, one that I have been hoping he might grow out of given his age and the behavior that one would expect of a respected businessman."

"And just what might that be, sir?"

"My brother likes to think he is a cowboy, sir."

"A cowboy?" Clarkson repeated, looking behind him to make sure that Martin was getting all of this down.

"Yes, sir, CAS—Cowboy Action Shooting? Surely you've heard of it. I'm lead to believe it's immensely popular."

Clarkson now turned fully to his young assistant and raised his eyebrows in query. Martin nodded that he had heard of it.

"Yeah," the young agent confirmed. "Some kind of a fast-draw competition."

"I'm afraid that's not strictly true, sir," Stevens corrected him. "It's more of a fast, and accurate, *shooting* competition. Which, to be honest, I could live with if it weren't for the dressing up."

"Dressing up?" Clarkson asked.

"Yes, sir, apparently it's simply not good enough to be able to shoot like a cowboy. It would seem that it is also necessary for one to *look* like one too."

"So, let me get this straight. Your brother travels all over the country to take part in these Quick Draw McGraw competitions and dresses up like Rooster Cogburn to do so?"

"Something like that, sir. Although, to be fair, Sean was never really that taken with the late Mr. Wayne. I would say his theatrical costumes lean more toward Charley Waite than the illustrious one-eyed marshal. You see, Mr. Clarkson, I too have an affinity for the old American West, only I choose to confine myself to watching interpretations of it rather than attempting to re-enact it."

Clarkson was impressed. He smiled at the old Brit, and just to show the Charley Waite reference was not lost upon him, he shot back. "Yeah? I would've thought, given your brother's age, that a Boss Spearman get-up would have been more in keeping."

Behind him Martin was rolling his eyes, obviously unhappy that all his boss and the old guy behind the counter seemed to want to do was to swap friggin' movie trivia.

As though picking up on Martin's agitation, Clarkson went back into business mode. "Mr. Stevens, does your brother own a .22 caliber pistol, do you know?"

"My brother owns several pistols, Mr. Clarkson," Stevens replied. "Though I doubt whether any of them would be of such a small caliber. I could easily find out for you. Sean keeps an inventory of the guns he owns, along with the firearms themselves, locked away in our gunroom."

"Sir, we would very much like to have a copy of that inventory, and also a look at the firearms in question. Might I suggest that you shut up shop until we are done? We would also very much appreciate any recent photos of your brother that you may be able to provide."

"Am I to take it then, gentlemen, that my brother is suspected of being involved in some kind of criminal activity?" Stevens asked.

"I think you already know the answer to that question, sir," Clarkson answered.

Five minutes later, they were in the shop's secure gunroom, which bore more than a passing resemblance to a bank vault.

Stevens led them across to the far corner of the room to yet another steel door, and sorted through his keys before finally finding the right one. He opened the door, and all three men stepped inside.

This inner room was much smaller, but there were still an impressive number of both long guns and handguns mounted in racks around the walls.

As well as containing the gun collection, the rear wall of the room formed a long work bench, complete with reloading press and a great variety of re-loading equipment—powders, brass cases, bullet heads and primers etc.—stacked neatly on the shelves in back.

"This is my brother's private collection," Stevens told them, sweeping his arm around to indicate the numerous firearms.

"Sir, are you telling us that all of these firearms belong to your brother Sean?" Clarkson asked.

As was to be expected, given Sean Stevens' hobby, there was a large preponderance of lever-action and other Old West type rifles and carbines, along with some vintage-looking revolvers and shotguns.

In answer, Stevens merely nodded.

Clarkson and Martin both began to walk around the small room, stopping frequently to lean in and admire a particular item.

Clarkson stopped in front of a pristine-looking Winchester 1897 pump-action shotgun. He turned to Stevens. "May I?"

"By all means," Stevens replied.

Clarkson picked the piece up and racked the action—it was as smooth as butter. "Is this thing an original?"

"Oh yes indeed, sir," Stevens answered. "My brother does have some working replicas. There are a couple of Italian firms that do some really excellent, historically accurate copies, but that is indeed an original Winchester."

Clarkson de-cocked the gun and placed it back in its rack before continuing his survey of the small room.

Stevens meanwhile busied himself with a small inventory book that was sitting atop one of the work surfaces close to the door.

After a minute or two, he made his pronouncement. "As I suspected, gentlemen, my brother does not own a .22 pistol."

Clarkson turned from his examination of what seemed to be an original Sharps cavalry carbine, and turned to look at him. "But you do have pistols of that caliber for sale?" he asked.

"Why yes, we have three or four that I can think of."

"Mr. Stevens, I note that there are one or two gaps in the racks," Clarkson said, suddenly changing tack. "Do you think you might tell us what particular items are missing?"

Stevens came across from the doorway and stopped for a moment to examine the empty space in the middle of the long gun racks. Clarkson was quick to pick up on the puzzled frown that quickly flitted across the man's face.

"Something wrong, Mr. Stevens?" he asked.

"No, it's just—well, it's not exactly a rifle that one could describe as 'Cowboy Action,' as it were," Stevens said.

"No? Then what exactly is it?" Clarkson pushed.

"It's a sniping rifle. An M-21 of Vietnam War vintage, to be more precise. And quite a valuable one at that."

"Maybe your brother took it to make a sale," Martin ventured.

"Not that rifle he wouldn't have," Stevens responded. "There are quite a few long guns in his collection that Sean might pass on for the right price, but that isn't one of them. It has great sentimental value to him."

Clarkson brought his attention to the vacant spaces on the wall where a set of unoccupied brass pegs bore testimony to the fact that a couple of short guns were also missing.

Again, that fleeting frown of puzzlement appeared upon Stevens' face.

"I take it we're not missing a brace of cowboy pistols either then?" Clarkson guessed.

"On the contrary, sir. The missing items are the very personification of the cowboy era. They are a matched pair of Colt Single Action Army revolvers, more commonly known as Peacemakers, in quite excellent condition and dated 1880," Stevens said.

"And yet you weren't expecting to see them missing," Clarkson ventured. "Why is that?"

"Well, those particular pistols are very collectable. As I said, they are in really quite excellent condition and would easily fetch up to twenty-thousand dollars each, probably more if sold as a matched pair. They are not the kind of pistols that one would shoot at all, let alone use in a CAS competition. As I said earlier, there are some very fine Italian reproductions out there at quite affordable prices. These are my brother's Cowboy Action shooters." Here, he turned to indicate a very authentic-looking pair of modern reproductions of the venerable SAA. They were Uberti Cattleman El Patron revolvers in .45 Colt caliber, both with four-and-three-quarter inch barrels. As he stepped closer to indicate the guns, Clarkson caught, again, the same puzzled look flit across Stevens' face.

"How very odd," Stevens murmured, more to himself than the two agents.

"Something wrong, Mr. Stevens?" Clarkson asked once again.

"Well, it's just that his competition guns are still here," Stevens said, "but his rig is missing."

"Rig?" This time, it was Martin who voiced the question.

"His gunbelt and holsters, sir," Stevens answered. "It's a very fine rig. My brother had it custom made for himself by John Beattie of Scotland the last time he was over in the UK. I can't imagine why he would take it with him when both of his competition guns are still here."

By this time, Clarkson was over at the reloading bench. He bent to the simple Lee turret press and removed the set of dies that were in place. He brought the dies closer to his face until he could make out the legend stamped into the shank of one of them—Lee .45 Colt.

"What caliber did you say those missing Colts are?" he asked Stevens.

"They are both Colt .45s," the Englishman said.

After Stevens had confirmed that there were no more firearms missing from the racks, they made their way back into the store's main area.

"Will this take much longer, agent?" Stevens asked. "I do have a business to take care of after all."

Clarkson turned around to look through the store's glass doorway. "I appreciate that, sir," he said, swinging back to face Stevens. "But there doesn't seem to be a queue forming out there, and we do have a couple more points to cover. That recent photo of your brother, for one. Do you think you might have one or two that we might use?"

Stevens sniffed and favored Clarkson with a good five seconds worth of "the look" before turning on his heels and making his way into the back office. He was back within minutes, proffering a framed 8x10 to Clarkson. "From my brother's work desk," he said as he handed the photograph over.

"You're shitting me!" Clarkson said as he inspected the image.

"Believe me, sir, I wouldn't dream of doing such a thing," Stevens responded. "Neither myself nor my brother are married. Therefore, the family gatherings and social events that we are called upon to attend are so few and far between that they are practically non-existent. That, so far as I am aware, is the most recent photograph of my brother Sean."

Clarkson ran a hand across his lower face as he continued to study the photograph.

Martin came up from behind to take a look over his shoulder. "Holy shit! It's Two-Gun Tex of Texas!" he said, snorting with laughter.

Clarkson could not suppress a smile himself. The photo depicted a small, elderly guy wearing spectacles and dressed up to look like a Western desperado.

With a high-crowned cowboy hat perched on his head, and carrying a large, pump-action shotgun to augment the brace of pistols that he wore in a wide leather gunbelt at his waist, he was staring into the camera, putting his all into a steely-eyed glare of challenge and defiance. This had the overall effect of making him look like a small, bespectacled old guy in cowboy fancy-dress.

"This really the best you can come up with?" Clarkson asked.

"Well, you did stipulate recent," Stevens said, sounding a little annoyed. "There are other photographs, but none as recent. You'll find a few dotted around the walls, including that one to your side." With a nod of his head, Stevens nodded to a framed black-and-white that was mounted on the wall a foot or so off to Clarkson's side.

Clarkson passed the photo he had been holding back to Martin and stepped nearer to investigate.

The print showed a much younger version of the old guy in the cowboy picture, standing alongside and shaking hands with a tall, lean-framed man who looked to be maybe ten years older.

Both men had their arms draped around each other's shoulders, and both were smiling happily into the camera.

"That was taken at Camp Perry some years ago," Stevens commented. "It's not very often one sees Sean looking so happy. I guess he had good reason to that day. He had just won one of the national long-range shooting competitions and then had one of his heroes come across to personally congratulate him."

Clarkson turned to Stevens and raised an eyebrow.

"The other gentleman in the picture, sir," Stevens elaborated. "That is Gunnery Sergeant Carlos Hathcock, of the US

Marine Corps. One of the Corps' most celebrated snipers. He was active in the Vietnam War and achieved a confirmed record of 93 kills. Back then confirmed kills had to be witnessed by a third party officer. Hathcock and his spotters estimated that the true number of his kills was more in the region of three hundred, including a North Vietnamese Army commanding general. He is usually best remembered for the feat of shooting an NVA sniper who was just about to shoot him. Hathcock's bullet passed clean through the enemy sniper's scope and into his eye."

"Hey, I saw that movie!" Clarkson exclaimed. "Tom Berenger, right?"

"I believe they did make a film based on Sergeant Hathcock's experiences sir, yes," Stevens answered.

"Well, I'll be," Clarkson said. "So your brother actually out-shot this guy?"

"On no, sir. Sergeant Hathcock was not shooting that day. He was there to hand out some of the trophies. He was so impressed with Sean's achievement, though, that he came over to personally congratulate him. As I say, Sean had just won an impressive long-range match."

"Yeah?" Over what distance?" Clarkson asked.

"One thousand yards."

"Jeez that's over half a mile!" Martin exclaimed.

"Indeed it is, sir," Stevens concurred.

"I guess the target must be somewhat barn-sized, huh?" Clarkson said.

"Not quite, sir. The overall target is six-foot square, but the black circle is only forty inches diameter and the ten-ring a mere twenty inches."

"Yeah? That must have been quite a scope your brother was using," Clarkson said.

"Oh no, sir, you misunderstand. The competition my brother won that day was for iron sights only, no scopes allowed. Sean was using a very fine Pedersoli rifle—a Sharps Long Range in .45-120 with a tang-mounted Creedmor sight in place."

Clarkson took a minute to digest this, trying to imagine what a six-foot high target would look like at half-a-mile distance. He finally doubted that he could actually *see* such a target at that range.

"Hell, no wonder the old gunny was impressed," he said.

"Yes indeed," Stevens agreed. "Sergeant Hathcock caught up with Sean just as he was about to shoot in one of the Service Rifle stages. Sean prevailed upon him to autograph the stock of his M-21, which the sergeant did in indelible marker. That's the rifle that Sean has with him at the moment. As I said earlier, it's not one that he's likely to part with."

While they had been talking, Martin's cell phone had gone off, and after checking the caller ID, he had retreated to the far side of the store to answer it. He paced around as he listened to the caller, growing more and more restless and agitated as the call went on. Finally, he slipped the cell back into his pocket and gestured frantically for Clarkson to join him.

"We need to finish up here, boss, and quick," he told Clarkson in a rushed, excited tone as Clarkson came across to stand next to him. "That was central office. They've just got word of a drug deal in Detroit that went pear-shaped in a major friggin' way. Happened just yesterday. They got five dead at the scene, all male, all gunshot fatalities. Ballistic reports have just come back, and it ties one of the fatalities directly in with our own investigation. One of the dead guys was shot at close range with a .22 pistol—the same friggin' one that put Connor's brains all over his apartment wall."

"Oh yes!" Clarkson exclaimed.

"That ain't all though, boss," Martin continued, his eyes shining brightly with excitement. "Get this—three of the deceased were shot with a high-powered rifle. All one-shot kills. All at a range of almost a thousand yards!"

"Sweet baby Jesus!" Clarkson whispered.

Chapter Seventeen

They stood at the edge of the low parapet of the multi-storey, looking out across the windswept wasteland—Clarkson, Martin, and a local PD lieutenant.

The three small, red flags that had been affixed to six-foot high wooden stands were just visible in the far distance, fluttering like crazy in the strong wind. Each flag marked the position of one of the rifle-shot bodies.

"The tech guys measured it out," the lieutenant—a young up-and-comer by the name of Hendriks—said. "Closest one—the one who was behind the wheel of the pickup—is eight hundred and fifty yards away. The other two are a little further out, eight hundred and eighty yards or so."

Clarkson smiled to himself. It was bang on a half mile.

"Guy up here must have been using some kind of high-powered rifle with a very good scope," Hendriks continued. "Hell, we got boys on our SWAT team couldn't make a shot like that once, never mind three in a row."

Clarkson felt like saying, *"Scope? Our boy don't need no steenking scope!"* But he let it pass.

"He didn't pick up his brass afterwards," Hendriks said. "Which is kinda dumb, I guess, seeing as it will be a positive tie-in to the rifle when and if we find it."

Clarkson wished he had that brass in the palm of his hand right now. It would be nice to jiggle it up and down while he looked out onto the distant plain below, playing the role of El Segundo.

"Sharps. Or some kind of buffalo gun. He can shoot. And we have lost five more!"

Barton Heyman. The actor's name came easily to him. It was one of his favorite movies, and had given Burt Lancaster some of the finest one-liners of his acting career. He smiled to himself as he remembered the confrontation between Valdez and El Segundo.

"Ever hunt buffalo?"

"Apache."

"I knew it. When?"

"Before I know better."

Now that right there was some great Goddamn screenwriting.

"I think our boy reckons he'd make a damn fine Bob Valdez," he said, more to himself than to the other two, who just exchanged puzzled glances with each other. "And you know what?" Clarkson added. "I think at this point I'd have to friggin' agree with him. Jesus, that surely was one fine piece of shooting." He turned to face the young lieutenant, who was obviously a little taken aback by Clarkson's statement. "What about the other two?" he asked.

"Well, we got one down there right in the middle of everything," Hendriks said. "We think that guy was just a chemist brought along to test the product, classic case of wrong place wrong time. The other one was right there in back of us." He turned about to indicate the paint-sprayed outline on the concrete floor. "Male, negro, shot through the left eyeball at very close-range with a .22 caliber pistol—the same pistol, as it happens, that was used on one of your victims. The guy has known connections to the Redbone family, one of their known enforcers. Of course, Mr. Redbone denies all knowledge of him and any of the other victims. He was found in possession of a Colt Python in .357 mag—one shot fired, no evidence as to where. We got no blood stains on the ground, so it's unlikely that he hit the shooter. That's a nice piece of ordinance to just be leaving behind, though. Surprised your guy didn't take it with him."

Clarkson wasn't, but said nothing.

"There was some real serious firepower found down there at the deal site as well. Little guy we figure was a chemist was chopped practically in half with a Colt Commando. The weapon in question was found still in the truck along with the dead driver, whose prints are all over it. He's our closest rifle hit. Also in the truck was an unfired Uzi. One of the others taken out with the rifle was toting a friggin' Desert Eagle in .50 AE caliber. Makes Dirty Harry's gun look like a .38 Special. Just three rounds left unfired. The other one was carrying a Glock 17 with just one round left unfired. It's fairly obvious they were aiming at the pickup—we got quite a few corresponding hits in the bodywork. The little chemist guy wasn't armed." Hendriks paused in his report to consult his note book.

"Drugs wise, we got three kilos found in the truck and another one lying alongside the chemist. No money." He flipped a couple of pages. "Evidence of another vehicle out near where Mr. Desert Eagle and Mr. Glock were lying—some kind of SUV from what little tracks we got, but nothing specific. Best calculation is that we had at least one survivor, who managed to use the vehicle to get away under fire, probably along with any money that was involved. Good news is we got some fine prints from both the Uzi and the interior of the Bronco. Didn't take long to pull a match. He's a pretty bad dude with a long, serious sheet. It's all in the file." He handed over a slim folder, and Clarkson opened it up. He looked at the mug shots on the first page, and couldn't prevent himself from laughing out loud.

"Jesus Christ on a friggin' pogo stick!" he exclaimed, the laughter still bubbling from his lips. "We got ourselves a real friggin' game of Cowboys and Indians being played out here."

Chapter Eighteen

They were back in the city of brotherly love.

Clarkson sat in a bedside chair, only feet away from the tiny, frail figure that occupied the bed. The girl's small, delicate face was still covered in ugly bruises and her large, doe-like eyes—eyes that she constantly flicked across to her father sitting on the opposite side of the bed—were wide with wariness and alarm.

He had been granted access to the young girl's bedroom with extreme reluctance on the part of her father.

"Police already come!" Tran Than Chinh had told him time and time again. "Daughter know nothing. Not remember nothing. She tell this already, many time."

Clarkson had prevailed and had finally won through, going into the girl's bedroom with her father, and leaving Martin to wait in the small living room.

The girl's name was Tran Thi Hue.

"Miss Tran—Thi," Clarkson began, his voice soft and gentle. "I'm not here to upset you, and I promise this won't take long, but we really do need your help, and in helping us, I think you'll be helping someone else that you know and care about." He pulled out the black-and-white photograph that he had cropped from the Camp Perry image given to him by Geoffrey Stevens. "Miss Thi, do you know this man?" He turned the photo around so that both the girl and her father could see it. There was an audible gasp of surprise from the father.

The young girl stared, wide-eyed, and nodded her head. "It is Uncle Sean," she whispered.

"And did Uncle Sean come to visit you recently?" Clarkson asked.

"Mr. Stevens come, yes—show respect. Nothing else,"

her father interjected. "She no well. Hurt very bad. Mr. Stevens bring flowers, gifts is all."

"Please, Mr. Tran, I need Thi to answer the questions," Clarkson told her father before turning back to the girl. "Did he come to see you, honey?"

Thi nodded her head, her wide eyes growing moist.

"And did he ask to see you in private, just you and him?"

Again, she nodded her head.

"Did he ask you questions? About the bad men who did the bad things to you?"

The young girl's lips formed a tight, thin line across her face and her breathing grew a little more rapid.

"Please, you need go now," Mr. Tran urged. "You upset daughter. Make her no well again."

Clarkson ignored him and carried on. "You knew one of them, didn't you, darling? One of the bad men. Sean knew that and he promised you something, didn't he, darling? Something the police could never give you. He promised to do something for you if you gave him the name."

The girl shook her head in denial and a fat tear trickled from her eye and rolled slowly down her cheek.

"Darling, you have to understand, these are very bad men, you already know that, and your Uncle Sean is in great danger from them. I want to help to protect him against these men. Did he promise you something, honey?"

This time, the girl gave a barely perceptible nod.

"My guess is he promised to find and kill the bad men for you if you gave him the name that you were too frightened to give to the police," Clarkson said.

There was another gasp of shocked surprise from her father.

"Did you give it to him, darling? Did you give him the bad man's name?"

Once again, the girl nodded, and her father muttered something in a stream of rapid, unintelligible Vietnamese.

"Miss Thi, I'm going to show you some pictures now, and I need you to be very strong for me. Can you do that, honey?"

"Please, no more. You have to…" Mr. Tran began, but Clarkson whirled on him and cut him off with a hard stare.

"I look," Thi said in a tiny whisper.

"I need you to tell me if these are the men that attacked you, okay, honey?"

She wiped a tear away from her cheek and nodded.

He took the three mug shots out from his pocket and showed her the one of Farrell. She gave a strangled sob, and her tiny hand flew to her mouth.

"Was he one? Was he the one you knew?" She nodded, still sobbing, and Clarkson showed her the photo of Connor. She closed her eyes and nodded again. "Just one more, darling. I need you to be brave, okay?"

She opened her eyes again, and he showed her the Indian. Again, she nodded her head.

"Were there anymore?" Clarkson asked.

She shook her head no.

From the far side of the bed, her father, tears running from his own eyes, spoke up. "You catch these men!" he exhorted. "You catch and punish, yes?"

"We might catch one of them, Mr. Tran," Clarkson told him. "And if we do, I'll certainly do my best to see to it that he's punished. The other two have already been punished." He took hold of the photos of Farrell and Connor and tore them in half. "These two are dead."

"Karma," Tran whispered. "I know now why I am there that day to save his life—karma. Mr. Stevens a good man for doing what he do."

"Sir, I'm afraid the police won't see it that way. They'll be looking to punish him for what he's done."

"Mr. Stevens good man!" Tran repeated. "Should be given medal for what he do."

Clarkson couldn't really find it within him to offer an argument.

"Well?" Martin asked as they pulled away from the house.

"She confirmed it," Clarkson said. "It's Stevens alright. The Indian's the last one."

"So the little Viet guy is just like the undertaker in the *Godfather*, huh?" Martin said. "Going to Stevens to seek revenge for his daughter's rape. You know, I had a lot of respect for Don Vito in that movie, but I always figured he wimped out a little not having those fuckers whacked."

"Hey, that's not bad," Clarkson smiled. "We'll make a movie buff out of you yet. Couple of things wrong with your statement, though. The undertaker's daughter—his name was Bonasera by the way—did not get raped. She got badly beaten up because she wouldn't come across. Also, you should never admit that you were rooting for the bad guys in that movie. Guys like us are supposed to be spending every waking hour putting fuckers like Don Corleone and his family out of business. Not your fault. It's that prick Coppola. He made friggin' heroes out of the Goddamn Mafia, for Chrissake. Too bad he didn't make it a few years earlier. What McCarthy would have made of that cocksucker is anybody's guess. Anyway, in answer to your question, no, I don't think Tran did approach Stevens. In fact, until about ten minutes ago, I don't think he knew a damn thing about what Stevens was up to. Now that we know he's definitely involved, though, we need to turn things up a notch. Soon as we get back, put out a nationwide APB on him. We need to get hold of all his credit card details and see if we can track him through his spending. Run a check on airline tickets and hotel reservations, anything where he'd need to show some ID. I'd like to think that this guy isn't a major player and doesn't have access to multiple IDs."

"For someone who ain't a major player, he isn't doing too badly," Martin observed, somewhat dryly. "He's already taken out six guys that we know about, some of whom most definitely *were* major players according to Hendriks. And we can't be certain that he hasn't already taken out the Indian. Who's to say that it wasn't him driving away in the SUV with the Indian's body in back? They found one more brass case than there were rifle kills up in the parking lot, don't forget."

"I don't think so," Clarkson said. "I think if Mr. Wolf Eyes had been killed or wounded out there, the local techies would have found some blood evidence to support it. No, I think that the extra case was our boy's one and only miss. I'm betting that at that point, Jimmy boy wasn't making it too easy for him by playing statues. Make sure we get a Federal APB out on the Indian too, by the way. I want everything that anyone has on him—favorite haunts, known associates, everything. If we find the Indian, I'm willing to bet our friendly neighborhood cowboy won't be too far behind."

"That's if we get to him first," Martin said. "Our cowboy seems to have some tracking abilities of his own. Plus, I don't think Stevens is gonna be the only one looking. If Hendriks was right, then it means that our red-hued friend has made away with a tidy bundle of that nice Mr. Redbone's cash while Mr. Redbone himself has exactly zilch in the way of product to compensate him, and I don't know about you, but I get the distinct impression that Mr. Redbone ain't the sort of guy who likes to get short-changed on a deal."

Chapter Nineteen

"We got something, boss." Martin was obviously excited as he came into the office and kicked the door closed behind him.

Clarkson lifted his head from the sheaf of reports he had been studying and waited for the news.

"A hit on Stevens' credit card." Martin smiled as he waved a thin sheaf of papers in front of him. "He used it a few days ago in Detroit to rent himself a car. The good news is he's still got the car, hired it for a full week. The best news is the vehicle has a built-in GPS tracking system."

"Make the arrangements," Clarkson said, coming out of his chair in a rush. "We're going back to Motown."

Not for the first time, Sean Stevens cursed out loud as the rental car plunged into and out of another huge pothole. He realized now that he should have rented some kind of 4x4, but at the time he had picked up the vehicle, he had no anticipation of having to drive anywhere except within the city limits.

At the moment, he was about as far removed from the city's outskirts as it was possible to be—way out in the boonies, in the wild, wooded hill country that lay to the north.

He had been driving up and down a collection of rough country roads and even rougher dirt and gravel tracks since early that morning, and the sun—the little that could be seen of it behind the great mass of gunmetal clouds that rolled and drifted across the sky—was now well past its nooning and moving on into late afternoon.

He was following the signal of the Mini GPS global satellite tracking device that he had surreptitiously attached to the Indian's Harley some days previously while it had been parked outside the Hog Roost bar.

His brother, Geoffrey, would have been amazed to see him reacting to the information transmitted via a brand new cell phone that he had mounted to the dash of the rental car.

He consulted the map displayed on the cell's screen once again, and the small red dot that corresponded to the bike's position. He pulled over to the side of the dirt road and brought the car to a halt. The red dot, which seconds before had been flashing, indicating movement, had now changed to a static display, indicating that the Harley, and the Indian riding it, had come to a halt. He waited a full ten minutes, his eyes glued to the cell's small display screen. The red dot retained its constant glow, and did not shift from its location on the map. It looked as though the Indian had finally arrived at his destination.

Sean picked up the cell and zoomed in on the dot's location. As the scale of the map diminished, he could now make out another smaller track, branching away from the dirt road that he was currently on.

He started the car moving again, keeping in low gear and making slow progress toward the cut-off up ahead.

Without the cell phone map to guide him, he would have missed it completely. Indeed, even with the map, he came awfully close to driving right past. This was hardly surprising, for the muddy trail that branched off from the dirt road at a near right-angle was narrow in the extreme and flanked with heavy foliage on both sides.

Sean stopped the car just past the turnoff and got out. He left the engine running and made his way back to the narrow gap in the trees and bushes. There had been rain recently, and the tracks of the big motorcycle could easily be identified in the freshly churned mud. He followed the tire tracks in for about twenty yards and then came up against a crude barrier that stretched across the track. The simple gate, no more than a narrow triangle constructed from heavy, galvanized bar that was hinged to an upright bar on the left and padlocked to a second upright on the right, had proven to be no obstacle for the Harley. Sean could see the tracks in the soft earth where the bike had simply skirted around the right hand upright and through the gap between it and the nearest tree.

It would, however, he knew, prove more than capable of halting the rental car. It was immaterial anyway. Even without the gate in place, he had no confidence in the car's ability to successfully negotiate the narrow, slippery downward-sloping track beyond. He would have to park up here and go in on foot.

He made his way back to the car and to the equipment in the trunk that he knew he would shortly need.

Jimmy brought the bike to a stop and turned off the ignition, hauling back on the handlebars to engage the kick-stand.

Before the low growl of the big engine had faded completely away, three men had exited from the low-walled log cabin in front of him and were standing on the building's rough-hewn timber porch. All three wore motorcycle Color jackets along with an impressive collection of both arm and facial tattoos. Two of the men carried long guns, one of them a Remington 870 pump-action shotgun, and the other a boxy, crude-looking piece of equipment with a huge drum magazine attached to it. The latter weapon looked like some kind of assault rifle. Jimmy Wolf Eyes knew, though, that it wasn't. He knew that what he was looking at was one of the most destructive handheld weapons that had ever been invented. It was an AA-12 automatic shotgun. The weapon had been extensively modified from an earlier design—the Atchisson Assault shotgun—and had a strictly military-only designation, making it illegal for civilians to own.

The tallest of the three men stepped down from the porch and began making his way toward where Jimmy stood alongside his bike. The guy would have made a damn fine Viking. He had the build and the muscles, along with the flowing blond locks and long, plaited beard. Unlike his two companions, he was not carrying a gun himself, but there was a semi-automatic pistol of some kind riding high on his waist. He stopped when he was still some ten yards or so away from Jimmy.

"Jimmy Lobo Eyes!" It was practically a snarl. "You a long way off the reservation, man. What the fuck brings your ugly Apache butt out here?"

"I thought I'd drop by and see whether you're still taking it up the ass," Jimmy replied.

The big biker gave a deep frown and strode across the gap between them. He came to a halt when they were practically face-to-face, and then his tattooed face broke into a huge, toothy grin as he opened his arms wide and threw them around Jimmy. Jimmy responded in kind, and the two men indulged in a mutual bear-hug.

Finally, the big biker stepped back, still grinning through his drooping moustache and beard.

Jimmy wasn't much in the way of a grinner. His lips curled slightly upwards in what for him was a winning smile. "Good to see you, Cole."

"So, what gives, man?" the other man said. "I'm guessing you ain't out here to socialize, huh? If you are, you're apt to be a mite disappointed. They's a couple of bullfrogs down by the creek with a more interesting conversational output than ol' Rodney and Earl here." He threw a hand back to indicate the two bikers on the porch, and Jimmy threw a nod in their direction.

"Howdy, boys."

They both nodded back, and the one holding the AA-12 leaned over the porch to spit a stream of tobacco juice into the weeds that lay beyond. "Jimmy," he muttered by way of greeting.

"Earl ain't usually so chatty," the biker named Cole informed Jimmy with a grin. "He's feeling a mite excited, though, account of him just getting hisself a brand-new toy."

"So I noticed," Jimmy said, throwing a glance at the AA-12. "So, the Russians came across then?"

"They sure did," Cole responded, "though only with a pair of the mothers for now. They weren't cheap, but once we get a dozen or so together, along with some of the specialist ammo they use, we'll be able to name our own Goddamn price. Hell, just about every damn prepper in the country will want one of those babies." He turned around to face the two men on the porch. "Earl, get on down here and show that thing to Jimmy."

The biker named Earl came down off the porch and shuffled toward them. He was big in every sense of the word, but most especially around the middle.

He stopped a foot or two away from Jimmy and held up

the shotgun for inspection.

"Fuck's sake, Earl, hand it over, willya?" Cole said, reaching over to pluck it out of the other man's arms. "We ain't gonna friggin' run away with it."

Somewhat reluctantly, Earl relinquished his grip on the weapon, and Cole took it from him and passed it across to Jimmy.

Jimmy hefted it appreciatively.

"That's one heavy piece, man" he mused, reckoning the thing must weigh all of fifteen pounds.

"That's mostly the ammo," Cole told him. "You got twenty rounds of 12-gauge sitting right there in the drum."

"Sure ain't gonna win no prizes for looking good," Jimmy said. "It's about the ugliest Goddamn gun I ever seen."

"Chrissake, Jimmy, ain't nobody asking you to fuck it!" Cole said. "Here, give it a try." He grabbed Jimmy by the shoulder and turned him around to face a bank of four McQueen figure 11 military targets that were stapled to plywood boards and mounted into the dirt about twenty yards away. He caught the half-sigh, half-snort of frustration behind him from Earl.

"Jesus, Earl, he ain't gonna break the damn thing!" he exclaimed to the obviously less than happy biker. He turned his attention back to Jimmy. "She's loaded with ordinary 12-gauge buck at the moment. We've got a couple of boxes of fin-stabilized FRAG 12. They're like mini-fucking fragmentation grenades and will reach out to two hundred yards. Can you believe that? Two hundred yards with a friggin' shotgun! We ain't about to let rip with those puppies on a set of plyboards, though. Not at the price them Russkies are charging for the damn things. Ain't no fire select except your own damn finger. Pull once for a single shot, pull and hold for full auto. So go ahead and get some. Don't worry about the recoil—there ain't any."

Jimmy swung the gun up into his shoulder, lined up on the nearest figure 11, and braced himself. The gun was heavy enough to soak up a lot of recoil, he knew, but he'd fired enough 12-gauges in his time to know it was still gonna kick, especially if he put the mother into full-auto.

He figured that Cole probably just wanted the pleasure of seeing him shoot a shitload of sky once the muzzle began to climb.

He pulled back the trigger and held it in place. The shotgun began to roar and spit out empty husks at an alarming rate. He held the muzzle on track, which was surprisingly easy to do, and began to sweep the line of targets. Four seconds later, the magazine was empty, and every single target was showing signs of major damage. One of them was cut practically in half, and most of the others were sporting great, splintered holes.

Jesus, Cole was right. The damn thing had practically no recoil whatsoever, allowing the shooter to hold it easily on target without any climb. Fuck, if only he'd had it with him when the deal went sour! That cock-sucking bald fucker with his friggin' hand cannon, along with the mouthy suit with him, would both have been blown out of their fucking socks.

Thinking of the recent disaster caused him to ponder yet again as to who might have been responsible for taking out both of Redbone's guys, along with that moron Mickey, and then trying to make it a clean card by homing in on him.

The only thing that made sense was that somebody had somehow gotten wind of the deal and elected to eliminate everybody on site and then make off with both the cash and the product. The only flaw in that theory was that he had heard the news bulletins after the event, and they were all saying the same thing—a large amount of narcotics had been recovered at the scene, left behind, in other words, by whoever had done the shooting.

He supposed the smart thing to have done would have been to contact Redbone afterwards, try to explain what had happened and offer to return the cash. The only thing was, he had worked hard for that fucking money, unbelievably fucking hard. From the supposedly simple hijack in Florida, which thanks to that fucking lowlife trigger-happy fuck-up, Farrell, had turned into a Goddamn bloodbath, through to the mess they had gotten into with the girl—again, all thanks to that fucking Irish degenerate—it had proven to be just one long and incredibly painful ball ache. The thing with Redbone should have brought everything back on track, and yet, it hadn't. It too had turned into a clusterfuck beyond measurement.

He was turning the piece over in his hands, unable to deny that despite its looks, it was a decidedly mean and totally functional piece of ordinance, when Cole reached over and took it back.

"Better give it back to Earl," he said. "I think it's about due to be breast-fed."

Earl stepped in to take the gun, dropping the drum from it as he made his way back to the cabin, no doubt in search of another box of shot shells.

"So, what brings you way out into the boonies, man?" Cole asked.

"Coupla things," Jimmy said. "If you got an extra bunk, I could use a place to lay up for a while. Things are kinda hot for me back in the 'D' right now, and second, I could use some more ordinance before I move on. I got the money for both."

"You ain't gonna need no money for a bunk, and found," Cole replied. "Hell, we thicker than that, ain't we? You will for the hardware, though. I ain't never given a piece away yet, and I ain't about to start now, not even for you, bro." He reached into the breast pocket of his Colors and pulled out a pack of smokes, flipping one halfway out and offering it to Jimmy. He took it and Cole lit him up while drawing another cigarette from the carton with his lips. Cole got his own smoke going and snapped his zippo shut. "Hell, Jimmy, how come you to need more iron, man? The last time you bounced out of here, you were carrying enough hardware to start a friggin' small war. Something you need to tell me, bro?"

Jimmy took a long drag on his cigarette and blew a steady stream of smoke from the side of his mouth. "Things just went to shit the way they can do is all," he told Cole. "I still got the Browning, gave the Diamondback to Connor. The Uzi and the Colt are gone, though. Right now John Law probably has both of them, along with a full fucking set of my paw prints."

This was obviously worrying news for Cole, though the man did his best not to show it. Jimmy knew that fuck-ups like this with pieces that he had supplied were the main reasons that he liked to lay most of his stuff off on the prepper community. Most of the guns Cole sold would lie around gathering rust and dust in some underground bunker or cellar somewhere, unused except for the odd practice bout, until the Apocalypse finally popped up on the calendar, or hopefully didn't—and that was just the way the man liked it. Guns that were actually used, especially in anger, could come back at him with a whole new meaning to the word recoil.

Cole smiled at Jimmy, though it was obvious that he did not feel much like doing so.

"Ain't no biggy," he said. "None of them pieces was traceable, not to me anyway. You didn't leave any talking heads behind with the ones you lost, did you?"

Jimmy knew what he was asking. "No," he replied, remembering the mess that Mickey's brains had made on the rear window of the Bronco. That was one head that was certainly all done and dusted with talking.

Cole nodded in satisfaction.

"Well, that's some good news at least."

Jimmy could sympathise with Cole being somewhat worried about the situation. Although he and the biker leader could always rely on themselves not cutting any deals against each other, he was aware that Cole didn't know jack shit about the reliability of the others. He would have been worried too in Cole's position.

"Let's retire to the drawing room, as they say," Cole said with a smile. "It's getting set to be colder than a witch's tit out here. We got some good coffee on the go and a bottle or two of Jack to liven it up with." He beckoned to Jimmy and turned toward the cabin, but Jimmy asked him to hold on a while and instead made his way back to the Harley.

He came back carrying a leather pannier satchel that he'd removed from the bike.

"You bring your laundry?" Cole asked.

Jimmy shook his head and tossed the satchel across. "Eighty grand," he said matter-of-factly. "Find somewhere safe for it, willya? Maybe I'll take one of them Grim Reaper shotguns off your hands when I leave."

Cole grinned as he slung the bag across his shoulder. He accepted the gesture for what it was: a mark of the utmost trust between them. "Come on," he said. "Let's go get on the outside of some of that Java 'n' Jack."

Chapter Twenty

Sean opened up the trunk and stood for a second looking at the contents laid out inside.

His gaze lingered for a minute or so on the long, narrow Gun Guard rifle case in what was claimed to be airline-proof polymer, although he could think of more than one domestic airline whose baggage handlers would probably see that as an out-and-out challenge. He thought about the M-21 that nestled inside it and looked around at the wood-filled terrain. Wherever the Indian was holed up, he was reasonably sure that he could get well within the rifle's striking distance and set himself up in a hide of some kind. He decided against it. The other two bastards had come to their ends knowing the reason for it. He wanted the Indian to have the same knowledge.

The whole ambush scenario back in the city had been a mistake, he now realized. He had no regrets about the loss of life he had been responsible for. He was more than certain that society could well sustain the loss of such lowlife garbage. Nevertheless, it had been a mistake, and one that he could now rectify.

He took of his plaid Mackinaw jacket and folded it carefully before laying it in the trunk.

There was a large canvas duffel lying alongside the Gun Guard case, and he opened it up and withdrew the gunbelt, complete with attached holsters, from within.

The rig was crafted from the finest English leather, and had been custom-built for him from his own design by the master leatherworker John Beattie of Scotland. He had designed the rig to be purely functional. There was no fancy stamping, silver conchos, basket-weave effect, or patterned stitching, and yet the sheer simplicity of it lent it an elegance that most fancy rigs could not match. The belt itself was a simple two-and-a-half inch wide strip of lined leather with a tapered billet and buckle strap at either end, and carried a pair of matching cut-away holsters. The leather of both holsters and belt had been dyed and then burnished to a deep, russet tan.

Sean picked the rig up and quickly strapped it on. He was right-handed, and the rig had been designed for one-handed use rather than a simultaneous double draw.

The right-hand holster was a straight-draw with the body of the holster pointing directly down his outer thigh, while the left side holster was a cross-draw, designed to be worn closer to the midriff rather than on the thigh and canting the gun away from the vertical and across to the right at an angle that would make it easier to be drawn by the right hand.

Next, he withdrew the old wooden pistol case from the bottom of the duffel and opened it up. Inside, nestled perfectly into the pistol-shaped indentations within the green baize interior, was a matched pair of Single Action Colts.

He withdrew the final item from the duffel, a plastic ammunition box, labeled simply ".45 Long Colt," and opened it.

He withdrew the first pistol from the custom-made box and eased the hammer back to half-cock, allowing the cylinder to rotate freely, then flipped open the loading gate to expose the chambers. Rotating the cylinder with his left hand, he slid one of the big .45 cartridges into each of the chambers. Finally, with all six chambers loaded, he closed the loading gate, carefully lowered the hammer, and slipped the revolver into one of the holsters at his waist. He then repeated the loading procedure with the second gun before slipping it into the other holster.

Sean left the Mackinaw where it was, and instead, reached further into the trunk and pulled out a well-worn canvas duster and a battered old Stetson. He carefully removed his spectacles and placed them on top of the rifle case, then pulled on the coat and eased the hat onto his head before closing the car's trunk and turning to make his way back to the muddy track and whatever lay at the end of it.

Chapter Twenty-one

The level of liquid in the bottle of whiskey had dropped considerably by the time they heard the first ping of the alarm.

All three of the resident bikers stopped what they were doing and became instantly alert.

"What?" Jimmy Wolf Eyes asked.

"We got motion sensors and surveillance cameras in the woods and out on the track," Cole told him. "That's how come we were all ready and waiting to welcome you when you rode in."

"It's prob'ly just a deer," the biker named Rodney ventured.

"Check it out," Cole said to Earl, who was already reaching for the modified Atchisson.

The fat man got up from the large leather chesterfield he had been resting on—it was about the only piece of furniture in the place capable of accommodating his ample proportions—and, still clutching the shotgun, made his way to one of the side rooms.

"It ain't no deer," he sang out seconds later. "We got company."

"Shit!" Cole exclaimed, coming away from the large oak table that he and Jimmy had been sitting around.

For a brief second or two, he wondered if the Indian had set them up, and then immediately—and a little guiltily—discarded the thought. They had too much history behind them for that to be possible.

Still cursing, he came into the room where Earl was, with Jimmy close on his heels. It was a state-of-the-art surveillance center, with one entire wall of the small, windowless room given over to banks of electronic equipment and video monitors.

Earl said nothing, but tapped the screen of one of the monitors.

"What the fuck?" Cole responded as he leaned in to take a look.

Making his way, slowly and carefully, down the slippery track was a guy wearing some kind of long rain slicker and sporting a friggin' cowboy hat.

As they watched, the guy stopped to look up into the trees, and for a brief instant, they had a fair look at his face below the brim of the hat.

"You know him?" Cole asked, turning to Jimmy. Despite himself, he couldn't suppress the niggling doubt that the stranger's arrival had caused to surface.

"No. Why the fuck should I?" Jimmy shot back in anger, and then realized that Cole had a valid reason for asking, what with the stranger arriving so quickly upon his own heels. "I never seen him before, Cole," he added, the barb now gone from his tone.

"You think he might be one of Redbone's?" Cole asked. While drinking their coffee and Jack, Jimmy had given Cole the low-down on the fucked-up drug deal.

"Hardly," Jimmy said. "That guy sure don't look like a player. Jeez, he sure ain't no spring chicken, that's for sure, and I doubt if Redbone would send only one. Besides, how would they find me? I made damn sure I wasn't followed once I left the highway."

"Probably just some dumbass old hiker dude who got himself lost," Rodney ventured from behind them.

"I don't think so," Cole said. "If he's a hiker, where's his friggin' backpack?"

"You don't think he's one of them Ranger fellas, do you?" Earl asked. "Don't they'all wear them cowboy type lids?"

Cole nodded, knowing that some of them did. It still seemed decidedly unlikely, though. So far as he knew, and he had checked thoroughly, there were no wardens or Rangers operating anywhere near the area, which was one of the reasons why the site had been chosen in the first place.

"I tell you one thing," he finally said. "Whoever he is, he ain't gonna be walking back up that friggin' track again. We got too much at stake here to let that happen."

When he finally came down off the slippery track and into the small clearing at the bottom, Sean was not surprised by either the appearance of the cabin that stood on the far side of the cleared ground, nor the four men that stood out in front of it in obvious, if unfriendly, welcome.

He had known the Indian must have been making for a refuge of some kind, and several times while making his descent, he had caught the glint of sunlight reflecting off of glass high up in the trees, marking the spots were the cameras had been sited.

The men were arrayed in a line some twenty yards or so in front of the cabin. The two on either end were both cradling long guns. The two guys in the middle had both pulled their jackets out of the way to reveal the pistols that hung at their waists. One of them was the Indian, the other guy was big and muscled with long, blond hair and a beard that was plaited Viking style below his chin.

Sean began to make his way slowly and deliberately across the ground that separated them.

There was a concrete-filled oil drum positioned smack in the center of the clearing with an upright wooden flagpole set into the concrete. The flag that fluttered and snapped in the cold, wintry breeze was not Old Glory, though, and instead of stars and stripes, featured the Harley Davidson logo.

The flag the old man was looking at was one of Cole's most prized possessions. They had ridden onto the forecourt of one of the main Harley dealers in the city—four of them, all mounted on big Harley hogs and revving seven kinds of shit out of those big engines. The other three, Jimmy included, had sat on their bikes and continued to make noise while Cole dismounted, made his way to the forecourt flagpole, and calmly lowered the Harley flag that was flying there. He had folded the material in the same fashion as, and showing the same amount of reverence usually reserved for, the national flag, and then solemnly slipped the folded triangle inside his leather jacket before making his way back to his bike and to the waiting highway. Although there were plenty of startled faces looking out from inside the dealership, not a single person had ventured outside to challenge him.

The old guy had already passed the flagpole when Cole made some response to his presence.

"This here's private property, old timer," he called out.

The old guy did not respond, but simply kept moving forward toward them.

"Didn't you hear me, mister?" Cole called out again. "You can't be here. You trespassing, man. Who the hell are you? You lost or something?"

The man came on, carrying on walking until he was within twelve yards or so. "I'm not lost." His voice was calm and soft. "My name is Stevens. Sean Stevens. I have business here."

"Yeah?" Cole was genuinely puzzled. Had one of his contacts referred this old dude to him without even letting him know about it? If so, whoever it had been was going to be in a whole world of sorry for doing so. "So, who sent you?"

"Somebody in Philly."

"Mister, you gonna have to be a mite more specific than that," Cole said with a lot of hard bark in his voice now. "I know lots of people in Philly."

"A little girl sent me," Sean replied, his eyes fixed fast on Jimmy Wolf Eyes.

Cole glanced to the side, catching the look of surprise in Jimmy's eyes and the sudden tension in his jawline.

"My business here is with the Indian," Stevens sang out, his voice now surprisingly loud and clear. "The rest of you men can step back inside and sit things out if you wish to. In fact, I would strongly advise that you do so."

Cole couldn't prevent the laugh that escaped, and then the old guy switched his gaze to him, and the laughter died in his throat. "This some sort of fucking joke?" he snarled, angry at himself for letting the old fucker's stare unnerve him so.

"No joke," Stevens said, maintaining the icy stare. "If you think it's funny, why don't you make a trip to Philly, pay a visit to a little thirteen-year-old girl there who was viciously beaten, repeatedly raped in every orifice, and then beaten some more before being dumped in a trash container and left for dead. Have a word about it with her parents. Maybe you can get them to see the funny side."

Cole turned to the Indian beside him. "Jesus, Jimmy,

what the fuck did you do, man?"

"I'll explain later," Jimmy Wolf Eyes said. "It ain't like he said. Let's just get this done and I'll tell you after."

"You lying sack of dogshit!" Stevens spat out. "It's *exactly* like I said. Three of you against one poor, helpless child. The other two dirtbags have paid for it already—you're next." He flung back the side of the duster with his left hand and held it in place, revealing the angled butt of one of the Colts.

Jimmy Wolf Eyes would have laughed out loud at the antics of the crazy old coot standing there and bracing them all were it not for the look on his face and the words he had just spoken.

Farrell and Connor dead? Killed by this nut-job, Charles Bronson wannabe? It hardly seemed possible, and yet, how else had the fucker managed to track him down?

And then things began to click and tumble as they fell into place.

"It was *you*," he managed, his voice barely more than a croak as the revelation finally hit him. "Up there in the parking garage. It was fucking *you* sniping away. You that fucking ruined everything!" With a snarl of pure hatred, he began to claw for the Hi-Power riding on his waist.

Jimmy's frantic attempt to pull his pistol, the action that set everything else in motion, came as a complete surprise to his three companions.

But not to Sean Stevens.

Before Jimmy's hand had even closed around the Browning's grip, Stevens' Colt was out of its holster and up into the firing position, the hammer already hauled back into the full-cock firing position.

The old revolver roared, spitting out smoke, flame, and lead.

Cole, who was still turned slightly toward Jimmy, saw the look of shocked surprise that came to his friend's features as he staggered back toward the cabin, his hand still on the butt of the holstered pistol. In stark contrast to the white T-shirt that he wore, there was a small rosette of vivid red wetness in the center of his chest.

The flat barks of the old guy's pistol were still ringing out, and Cole realized with a flash of icy panic that the fucker was outgunning them all.

He whirled to his front, his right hand scrabbling for the

customised 1911 that he wore on his hip. "Nail the fucker!" he cried out, the frantic yell almost a scream. And then he began to scream for real as he felt the sledgehammer blows tearing into his chest.

Before the grip of the Colt had finished rolling in his hand under the recoil from the first shot, Sean's left hand had come quickly away from holding back the duster and up into play, reaching up to pull back on the revolver's hammer.

He began to pedal the action, keeping the trigger firmly held back as he cocked and released the hammer with his left hand over and over in rapid succession.

He swung the barrel of the gun along the line of targets in front of him as he did so. After putting the first round into the Indian's chest, he double-tapped both the guy with the pump and the big blond Viking, and then put the last of the six rounds into the chest of the biker with the impressive beer gut on the far right.

He tossed the empty Colt into his left hand and had the right-side gun out and ready to go before the left was back in its holster. He cocked and fired—one-handed this time—putting a second round into the fat biker's center of mass. The man grunted and began to sink to the ground, the large, ugly weapon that he had still been trying to bring into the fight, dropping from his hands as he did so.

All four men were now down on the ground, lying like rag dolls in an untidy line. Not one of them had gotten off a shot.

With the cocked Colt still in his hand, Sean made his way across to them. He came to the guy with the pump and reached down to pick the weapon up. Carefully de-cocking the Colt, he slipped it back in its holster. He eased back the Remington's handgrip slightly, just enough to confirm that there was a shell ready to go in the chamber. At the other end of the line, the fat biker was the only one still showing movement, his large body twitching and jerking upon the cold, hard ground. Sean approached him and saw that the man was trying to reach out to retrieve his fallen weapon—the bulky-looking long gun with a huge drum magazine attached. He walked closer to it and kicked the ugly-looking weapon away.

He made his way back to the center of the line then. The big blond guy was on his back, his eyes wide and staring sightlessly up into the late afternoon greyness, his neatly plaited beard now more scarlet than blond.

He switched his attention to the Indian. The man was lying with both hands clasped to his bloody chest, and was muttering something to himself over and over. He looked up to see Sean standing over him and his eyes cleared for a moment, burning brightly with hatred.

"You shouldn't have done what you did," Sean told him before placing the muzzle of the 12-gauge to the Indian's groin and pulling back on the trigger.

Chapter Twenty-two

The echoing boom of the shotgun had hardly faded away when Sean became aware of the unmistakeable noise of an approaching vehicle. He turned around to look back up the track. The noise grew louder—a big engine changing down through the gears—and then, around the curve at the top of the track, the vehicle itself suddenly appeared. It was a large black 4x4.

Sean let the Remington fall from his hands and walked a little way out into the center of the clearing, coming to a halt on the far side of the makeshift flagpole.

The big, truck-like vehicle came on, swerving from side to side as it negotiated the steep, slippery track.

He stood and watched as the car finally reached the level ground at the bottom of the track. It swerved violently to the left, coming to a skidding halt broadside on to him. All of the vehicles doors were flung open and men began to leap out.

One of them, tall and middle-aged, and wearing a long, dark overcoat, came running straight toward him. The three other occupants of the car sought shelter on its far side, drawing handguns and using the bulk of the 4x4 as a firing barricade.

The lone figure continued to advance toward him, the long skirts of his unbuttoned coat flying out behind him as he ran closer.

He was holding some kind of identity badge in his left hand, brandishing it before him as though it were a talisman to ward off evil. His right hand rested on his hip, clenched tightly around the grip of the pistol that was riding there.

"Federal Agents!" he yelled. "Do not move! Stay right where you are, Mr. Stevens."

Sean gave a flicker of a smile at the mention of his name.

His left hand went to the side of the duster and he slowly moved it back out of the way.

"No!" the agent advancing upon him shouted. "It's over! Put your hands up—now!"

Sean smiled. "It's not over yet," he whispered to himself. "Soon, though."

His right hand snaked down and across to the left, pulling the Colt out of the cross-draw holster in a swift, fluid movement born of many long hours of practice.

"No!" Clarkson screamed once again, pulling his Glock free from its holster.

Compared to the little old guy in front of him, his draw was molasses-in-wintertime slow. He skidded to a halt, dropping his badge into the dirt as he brought his left hand across to meet and steady the Glock.

He gave a mental *Oh shit!* as he found himself looking directly into the gaping bore of Stevens' six-shooter.

Shots were already ringing out from the men behind, none of them appearing to hit their intended target. Finally, the Glock came into contact with his left hand and he went into the classic two-handed Weaver stance that had been drilled into him many years ago.

The white dot of the Glock's foresight came on target, and he squeezed off two rounds in rapid succession.

He watched the figure in front of him shudder under the impact of the heavy slugs and go reeling backward, the gun he was holding flying from his fingers.

He walked slowly forward, the sights of the Glock still centered on the figure ahead. As the distance between them lessened, he saw Steven's legs give way and buckle beneath him, dropping his butt unceremoniously onto the hard-packed earth. The older man sat, splay-legged, his back up against the body of the rusted oil-drum and both hands thrust out to the sides for support.

Clarkson approached warily. He had seen the speed at which the old guy could move and had no intention of being caught unawares.

He stooped down, kneeling before the man he had just shot. Stevens' face was as colourless as the grey Michigan sky above. His eyes were glazed over in shock, and his breath was coming in great, ragged gasps.

Clarkson reached out, using the barrel of the Glock to

move the edge of the duster to one side. As he thought, there was a second Colt sitting securely in its fine leather holster. He reached across with his left hand and pulled it free. He turned the gun so that he could see the forward face of the cylinder. A look at the lead bullet heads that showed in four of the five chambers that were visible told him that the pistol was still very much loaded.

He cast a glance across to the gun that Stevens had let drop.

"I'm guessing that that one's empty?" he said to the wounded man.

Stevens nodded his head, coughing up bright red froth as he did so.

Clarkson swore softly to himself, realizing he had been duped into shooting a guy that had been pointing an empty pistol at him.

"Well, at least it wasn't a cigarette lighter," he said.

The reference was lost on Stevens.

The sound of running footsteps came from behind, and the next instant, Martin was there, pistol in hand and panting for breath.

"Jesus Christ, boss, that was some special kind of fucking dumb!" He gasped.

"Was that you shooting back there?" Clarkson asked.

"Me and the deputies, yes."

"You need to spend more time on the range, Joseph. I swear some of them slugs came closer to hitting me."

"Jesus fuck!" Martin shouted. "Why do you think we had such a hard time hitting the guy? You were right in the fucking way!"

"Yeah, well, hustle back there now and get the locals to call in some medical assist. See if they can hustle an air ambulance out here."

"You aren't going to need an ambulance," Stevens told him as Martin began making quick tracks back to the sheriff's vehicle. He looked down at his ruined chest and at the bright runnels of blood that were seeping out of both of the duster's cuffs.

Clarkson knew he was probably right—two chest hits from a .45 was usually enough for most people. He switched his gaze to the line of men lying in the dirt. "Did any of them even get off a shot?" he asked.

Stevens simply shook his head, too tired to make the words.

Clarkson shook his own head in wonderment.

"The fat guy on the end came close," Stevens admitted, his words little more than a hoarse croak. "The one with the weird-looking long gun. I was a tad slow, though. The extra recoil slowed me some. I loaded them old Colts up to near maximum pressure, and they took it too, shot beautifully for me." The talk took it out of him and he began to wheeze and cough again.

Clarkson waited for the fit to subside. "How long you got?" he asked.

Stevens looked down at the growing red stain. "Oh, about five minutes or so, I guess."

Clarkson gave a faint smile. "I meant before."

"Oh, six months or so, they say, maybe a year if I cut out damn near everything that makes life worth living. How did you know?"

"Your credit card history mostly. Couldn't help but notice all those medical payments, and then of course there was the knife and the brass you left behind. Not really the actions of a man who wants to evade the law."

"No, I guess not," Stevens admitted with another bubbling cough. "I guess it was the knife that took you to Philly, huh?" he managed to rasp once the coughing had subsided.

"That was some of it," Clarkson admitted. "But mostly, it was the movie."

"The movie?" Stevens asked.

"Yeah, you know, the one you copied—*Taken*? The thing with the electricity and everything."

Stevens looked at him for long, drawn out seconds, and then began to laugh—a laugh that soon turned into another wheezing, coughing attack. "Oh that's a bloody good one," he finally managed to rasp. "You tracked me because of a bloody picture show. A picture show I never even *heard* of let alone seen!" He began to laugh again, gouts of bright red blood frothing from his lips as he did so.

And why not laugh? It was a fine joke, Sean told himself. Hell, it was a joke that a person could literally die laughing at.

About the Author

Daniel was born and is still living in Liverpool , UK. He has a keen interest in military history in general, and a specific interest in the history of the Old American West.

He is a collector (and shooter) of Western period firearms, with a great interest in firearm history and development, and is also an avid participant in the popular sport of Cowboy Action Shooting.

Daniel has been (very happily) married for the last 40 years to his lovely wife Evelyn. They have been blessed with three strapping boys—Steven, Sean and Nathan (all now fully grown)—and with an incredibly loving, and lovable grandson—Liam.

Lightning Source UK Ltd.
Milton Keynes UK
UKOW02f1408130914

238532UK00002B/24/P